"What I've done to you isn't fair."

Chase placed his hands on Laura's shoulders and turned her around until she faced him. "You've got to trust me. Keith is my son, isn't he?"

"Yes."

He gathered her close, holding her, taking comfort in the palpitation of her heart against his chest. He'd suspected from the moment he'd seen the boy—Keith had the Sutton dark hair, dark eyes and a mischievous smile that reminded him of his brother Rafe.

He had a son. A boy. A beautiful, healthy child.

"If it means anything to you, I'm sorry," Laura said with a shuddering sigh. "But no matter what happens between us, for Keith's sake, we have to plan for his future."

"I want my son." The words came from his mouth without thought, came from deep in his core. Keith was a Sutton. He was family. Blood. And Suttons took care of their own....

Dear Harlequin Intrigue Reader,

It's autumn, and there's no better time to *fall* in love with Harlequin Intrigue!

Book two of TEXAS CONFIDENTIAL, *The Agent's Secret Child* (#585) by B.J. Daniels, will thrill you with heart-stopping suspense and passion. When secret agent Jake Cantrell is sent to retrieve a Colombian gangster's widow and her little girl, he is shocked to find the woman he'd once loved and lost—and a child who called him *Daddy*....

Nick Travis had hired missing persons expert Taryn Scott to find a client, in Debbi Rawlins's SECRET IDENTITY story, *Her Mysterious Stranger* (#587). Working so closely with the secretive Nick was dangerous to Taryn's life, for her heart was his for the taking. But when his secrets put her life at risk, Nick had no choice but to put himself in the line of fire to protect her.

Susan Kearney begins her new Western trilogy, THE SUTTON BABIES, with *Cradle Will Rock* (#586). When a family of Colorado ranchers is besieged by a secret enemy, will they be able to preserve the one thing that matters most—a future for their children?

New author Julie Miller knows all a woman needs is *One Good Man* (#588). Casey Maynard had suffered a vicious attack that scarred not only her body, but her soul. Shut up in a dreary mansion, she and sexy Mitch Taylor, the cop assigned to protect her, strike sparks off each other. Could Mitch save her when a stalker returned to finish the job? This book is truly a spine-tingling pager-turner!

As always, Harlequin Intrigue is committed to giving readers the best in romantic suspense. Next month, watch for releases from your favorite special promotions—TEXAS CONFIDENTIAL, THE SUTTON BABIES, MORE MEN OF MYSTERY and SECRET IDENTITY!

Sincerely,

Denise O'Sullivan
Associate Senior Editor
Harlequin Intrigue

CRADLE WILL ROCK

SUSAN KEARNEY

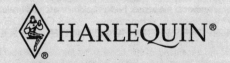

HARLEQUIN®

TORONTO • NEW YORK • LONDON
AMSTERDAM • PARIS • SYDNEY • HAMBURG
STOCKHOLM • ATHENS • TOKYO • MILAN • MADRID
PRAGUE • WARSAW • BUDAPEST • AUCKLAND

ISBN 0-373-22586-5

CRADLE WILL ROCK

This edition published by arrangement with Harlequin Books S.A.

® and TM are trademarks of the publisher. Trademarks indicated with
® are registered in the United States Patent and Trademark Office, the
Canadian Trade Marks Office and in other countries.

Visit us at www.eHarlequin.com

Printed in U.S.A.

ABOUT THE AUTHOR

Susan Kearney used to set herself on fire four times a day. Now she does something really hot—she writes romantic suspense. While she no longer performs her signature fire dive, she never runs out of ideas for characters and plots. A business graduate from the University of Michigan, Susan has written eleven novels and writes full-time. She resides in a small town outside Tampa, Florida, with her husband and children, and a spoiled Boston terrier. She's currently plotting her way through her next novel.

Books by Susan Kearney

HARLEQUIN INTRIGUE

*The Sutton Babies

Don't miss any of our special offers. Write to us at the following address for information on our newest releases.

Harlequin Reader Service
U.S.: 3010 Walden Ave., P.O. Box 1325, Buffalo, NY 14269
Canadian: P.O. Box 609, Fort Erie, Ont. L2A 5X3

THE SUTTONS

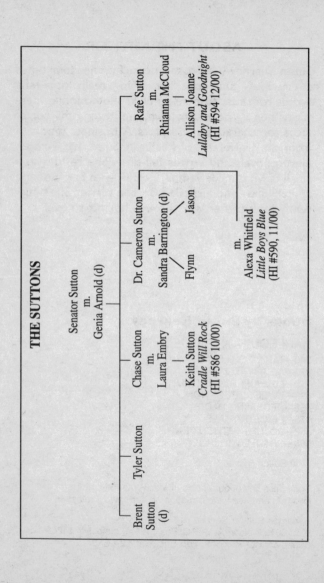

Senator Sutton
m.
Genia Arnold (d)

Brent Sutton (d)

Tyler Sutton

Chase Sutton
m.
Laura Embry

Keith Sutton
Cradle Will Rock
(HI #586 10/00)

Dr. Cameron Sutton
m.
Sandra Barrington (d)

Flynn   Jason

m.
Alexa Whitfield
Little Boys Blue
(HI #590, 11/00)

Rafe Sutton
m.
Rhianna McCloud

Allison Joanne
Lullaby and Goodnight
(HI #594 12/00)

CAST OF CHARACTERS

Chase Sutton—He'd lost his brother and his one true love all in one night. How will he react when he discovers he has a son he never knew he had?

Laura Embry—She left town running from a murder she didn't commit, and returns with a secret of her own.

Mark Bradley—He's an attorney defending Laura against double homicide, but is his past somehow connected with the Suttons?

Sally Walker—Bradley's secretary, and an ex-Sutton employee, she seems more interested in love than murder.

The Sheriff—He knows where the Sutton secrets are buried.

Francesca Martin—The police dispatcher is aware of more than she's willing to admit.

Lance Fuller—Is he an honest witness or a shrewd liar?

The Senator—Chase Sutton's father, very high-powered, very high profile—very much someone's target.

Judge Stewart—A man with his own agenda.

For Rebecca,
who helped in the beginning when I didn't know
sentences needed commas.
Thank you.

Prologue

Dust in her wake, Laura Embry drove through the wrought-iron double gates that marked the Suttons' vast spread and grinned, trying to picture Chase's expression when she told him her good news. His dark pupils would go smoky in a way that made her toes curl, his eyes crinkling beneath dark lashes that were long, dreamy. He'd toss her into the air, and…maybe they would explore the hayloft.

Earlier this evening, Laura's father had let her out of the evening ranch chores with a sparkle in his eyes, revealing his approval of Laura's romance with Chase Sutton. The two families had been friends and neighbors for years, and with Laura and Chase's newfound love for one another during the past year, the ties between the two ranching families could only deepen in the future.

Taking the left fork, she followed the painted white fence that led to the Sutton barn. Ten minutes later she parked the pickup. At her arrival, a gray-haired ranch hand looked up from the tractor engine he was working on, recognized her truck and tipped his Stetson. "Howdy, ma'am."

"Evening, Lance." Lance Fuller was hard of hearing, so she turned her face to answer him so he could read her lips. After she gave him a casual wave, he stuck his head back under the hood.

She entered the stable through a side door, the scent of horseflesh, hay and manure filtering to her along with soft knickers and snorts. Someone had already turned on the lights. At the thought that maybe Chase was here, her footsteps quickened. Unwilling to call out and disturb the animals, she strode down the center aisle, the click of her squared-toed boots muffled by fresh hay.

At the sight of a battered black Stetson peeking through the bars of a stall, her heart beat quickened. "Chase? Chase, I have good news."

The stall door opened and she stepped inside, ready to fling herself into Chase's arms. But it wasn't Chase. Brent, the eldest Sutton brother looked up from beneath his hat and surveyed her with a scowl.

Disappointment slowed her momentum. From a distance, her mistake had been easy to make. All five Sutton boys were dark-haired and dark-eyed like their mother, but Brent's eyes flickered with something threatening that made her uneasy. And she wondered if the rumors about him were true—that he had a drinking problem.

Unlike their famous father—the Senator who never drank alcohol—and Chase, who rarely sipped more than a single beer during an evening out, Brent's rugged features were slack from liquor. At the sight of her, his eyes lifted from the hot branding iron in his hand to settle on her chest with a speculative gleam.

Laura fought the urge to smack the leer off his face. Instead, she chewed on her bottom lip, tried to appear casual. ''Hi.'' An anxious hardness knotted her stomach. ''Is Chase here?''

Brent swayed on his feet, gesturing with the branding iron to a newborn foal. ''Just us and the horses.''

Brent wielded the branding iron toward a foal who backed awkwardly from the heat as if sensing danger. Chase had mentioned to her that his brother Rafe intended to tattoo the inside of the foal's lip— not devalue the animal's hide by branding it. Alarmed that Brent would go against his brother's wishes, worried that he could start a fire in the barn, Laura positioned herself between Brent and the foal.

She had no business questioning Brent's right to brand a Sutton horse. Still, she could no more stand by and do nothing than she could fail to help a lost child. ''Why don't we wait for Chase to help? He can hold her.''

She'd made the nonconfrontational suggestion, hoping Brent wouldn't take offense, knowing Chase would stop his brother's actions. But Brent's eyes turned sly as if he knew something that she didn't.

The Senator's eldest son stumbled forward, waving the brand, heedless of the possibility of a stray spark starting a fire. ''First I'm going to do the foal. Then…I'm going to do you.''

It wasn't so much his slurred words but the gleaming malice in his tone that simultaneously warned Laura and made her legs go weak behind the knees. Brent's broad shoulders and long reach prevented any hope of fleeing past him to escape. Backing protectively toward the foal, she grabbed a pitchfork from a neighboring stall and hefted it in front of her with both hands like a shield. "You're drunk, Brent."

"So?"

"So, I think we should put off branding the colt until you feel better."

"Fine. I can do you first." Brent advanced, a ruby ring strung from a chain around his neck winked at her with a demonic glow as he raised the fiery-red brand close enough to her face to singe her eyebrows. "Fight. Scream all you want, Lance won't hear you."

She was no match for Brent's strength, knew she had to keep her wits about her. "Chase—"

"Isn't coming. There's just the two of us."

Before she could think what to say, before she could decide to scream, he lunged at her.

She backed up.

Fear caused her to tighten her fingers around the pitchfork's handle. Brent stumbled forward, his face hard, his body tensed with pent-up violence.

The foal sidled away. Laura retreated until her shoulders struck the stall's rear wall. She could go no further. But Brent kept closing the distance between them, his breath reeking of whiskey, eyes shifty.

"Don't—"

With his free hand, he knocked off her hat, seized her hair, tried to yank her against him.

Ignoring the pain at her scalp, Laura tilted the pitchfork's sharp tines toward his chest. "Get back."

Brent dropped the branding iron, tried to catch it and tripped. Off balance, Brent fell, and the pitchfork's tines slid into his chest like a hook into a fish.

He swore, the vile stream of words spitting from his mouth like bullets. Releasing her hair, he staggered backward and looked down, eyes widening at the blood seeping through his sweat-stained shirt. With a grunt he collapsed and his weight pulled the pitchfork's handle from her hand.

Panic bubbled in Laura's throat. She half expected him to lunge back up and grab her. But he didn't move. She saw no sign of breathing.

Smoke burned her nostrils. Straw from the hot iron had caught fire. It took all her strength to grab a water bucket and douse the fire. She threw the rest of the water on Brent and then had no more energy to stop the shudders that gripped her.

"Wake up, Brent."

He didn't flinch.

"I mean it. Get on your feet, cowboy. Your chest wounds need cleaning before infection sets in."

He didn't stir enough to move one black hair on his head. He looked…lifeless. Not that she'd ever seen a dead person but she'd seen dead animals. He couldn't be dead.

Please, no. He couldn't be.

His unnatural stillness sent terror arrowing straight to her core. What had she done?

Gathering her courage, she leaned over Brent's body, felt his neck for a pulse. Nothing.

Oh, God! She'd killed him. She was a murderer.

Chapter One

New Orleans
Two years later

Finding Laura Embry had been as hard as trying to find a horse thief in heaven. The woman had quit Colorado for parts unknown and along the way lost her name, but Chase Sutton finally had her in sight on the crowded New Orleans street. She'd traded in jeans and cotton T-shirt for a cream skirt and jacket worn over a sky-blue blouse that made her look as sweet as a newborn kitten.

He knew better.

Her refined appearance hid a hellcat. Despite the severity of the coiled blond hair at her delicate nape, he recalled the lion's mane of silky hair loose and free across a pillow of blue columbine, the quicksilver taste of her eager lips, the softness of full breasts arching excitedly into his palms, the needy heat that kept his senses bucking as if he were trying to chin the moon.

Damn! He hadn't expected those long, lean legs or her proud posture to accelerate his pulse—not after what she'd done. While he'd never stopped hoping she was innocent, he should have known he couldn't toss off memories of happier times like old dishwater. She had a tidal wave of explaining to do—but he still couldn't believe she'd skewered his brother Brent for no damn reason. As much as Chase had loved Brent, he knew his brother had a tendency to violence and had some enemies. Maybe one of them killed him.

The Laura he'd known had been too warm, too even-tempered, too practical and forgiving to have done the unthinkable. Stubbornly, for two years, he'd refused to condemn her until he'd heard her story.

But then why had she sneaked out of town to avoid the law?

With her hat left in the stall, with her fingerprints on the pitchfork's handle and Lance placing her at the murder scene, Chase would have to be an idiot not to believe her guilty. And she'd made herself appear all the guiltier by taking a new name, settling in a new state.

She'd run away from him.

That's what hurt the most. In the worst trouble of her life, she hadn't come to him, but left him alone with his doubts. Alone with his anger.

He was soul-deep weary of questions that tore at his allegiance between his family and the woman he'd once loved, yet he'd never given up searching for her. For answers. For justice. For peace. He'd never depended on the authorities to find her. After burying his brother and spending twenty-four months making inquiries. He'd been no more successful than the police, but then he'd found her. Soon, he'd ask his questions.

Oblivious to the mesmerizing power she held over him, she walked into the courthouse. Her tempting mouth, small, with a light-pink gloss, challenged his restraint. She had a way of looking right into a man and making him think he was special. She'd fooled him, sure enough. Had she fooled Brent, too?

He followed, keeping his distance, and watched her speak to a clerk, receive a few papers and pay a cashier. He'd been planning a confrontation for too long to even think of surprising her in public.

He wanted privacy. An hour later, he found it. Stomach churning with anticipation, Chase trailed her into a vacant brass-walled elevator.

When he barred other passengers from joining them, Laura looked up from her courthouse papers and saw him. Alarm flared in her eyes. She dropped the folder. Tensed and tried to bolt. Too late.

After the elevator door closed, trapping them together, he waited for the car to rise a bit, then pressed the emergency stop button. He didn't say a word. He wanted her to speak first.

Her mouth opened and closed. He saw pain in her face and in her posture, like a woman who had lost all she valued, and he wondered how she could have walked away from family, home and him, without even a backward glance. She chewed her bottom lip, a habit he'd once found endearing. He had to give her credit. After her initial shock at seeing him again, she put surprise and fear behind her with several deep breaths, displaying a newfound control and maturity. Tilting her chin up and squaring her shoulders, she confronted him with an innate bravery he couldn't help but admire.

"How did you find me?" she asked, her words harsh, her tone bitter.

"Doesn't matter." Her coldness infuriated him and he answered in a matching vein.

And yet he felt her coldness was a cry of pain in itself. She couldn't even maintain the politeness of strangers. It wasn't like her to skip the social amenities. If the elevator door opened and she had an opportunity, she'd run before he could draw another breath.

Stuck, she grabbed his hand, squeezed hard and locked gazes with him, staring almost hard enough to seize the thoughts from his mind. Touching her again sent an odd sensation of pleasure through him, and he jerked away.

Color drained from her face. "You bring the law with you?"

He shook his head, unsettled by the vivid fear clouding her eyes, unnerved that the simple touch of her hand had made his heartbeat unsteady, furious at the gold wedding band he'd spied on her ring finger.

She'd married.

All his plans for this conversation washed away on a hot tide of resentment. He couldn't tell her how much that gold band on her finger hurt. He couldn't tell her that even after what she'd done, he'd always hoped they would get back together. He couldn't tell her how much he wanted to forgive her for leaving him.

As jealousy bit into him, his voice turned curt. "I thought it would be better if you turned yourself in."

Shoving back a stray lock of shimmering gold hair, she pushed away his suggestion at the same time. She shot him a look filled with unexpected compassion. "Why did you come after me?"

"You have to ask?"

The telephone in the elevator rang. They both ignored it.

But Laura's shoulders slumped—just a smidgen. Stress tightened her lovely lips. "I owe you an apology."

"For killing my brother?"

She flinched at his accusation, and he knew she was bleeding inside, but she faced him squarely. "I knew it looked like murder...."

"So you ran away."

"I panicked. Later I realized that running made me look guilty. I couldn't go back."

While she'd neither admitted nor denied her guilt, the secret hopes he'd been harboring began to drown. His gut-wrenching sense of wrongness was not proof of her integrity. For two years he'd run possibilities through his mind, thinking of ways she could be innocent. He'd considered that she'd witnessed Brent's murder and bolted before an unknown killer could hurt her, too. But from the way she'd refused to give him the facts, he knew he'd colored up the truth redder than a Navajo blanket.

She shook like a willow in the wind but didn't refute his accusation. Weary eyes that had seen death, the loss of her family and her home stared back at him with panic mixed with resolve. "I couldn't get a fair trial in Highview."

"A good attorney could have requested a change in venue."

For the first time, she avoided his gaze. "Even

moving the trial to another state wouldn't have been far enough.''

He planted his palms against the wall on both sides of her head, forcing her to look at him. ''Justice isn't a gift that is given, but one you fight for.''

Heat colored her tone. ''When's the last time someone took on the Senator and won? Your father's a powerful man.''

Her logical words tugged at him. If she was innocent, he could understand why fleeing had seemed like her best option. He knew his father and recognized his powerful connections. But the Senator was also a stickler for following the rules. He believed in the law. Chase's wealthy and influential father had a way of knowing everyone's business in Highview. He'd started as sheriff, became mayor, then governor before successfully running for his senate seat. The Senator had taken the death of his eldest son hard. He'd started to recover from the loss only when he'd begun grooming his second son, Tyler, to take over the ranch. The work had helped pull father and son out of their grief. And unlike Brent, Tyler seemed to thrive on the responsibility and hard work. Chase was proud of him.

They'd each dealt with the death of their eldest brother in their own way. The youngest, Rafe had finished law school but had ached to come home. He'd returned to the ranch to breed quarter horses, while Cameron, a medical doctor, had started a family in Boston.

Chase had considered quitting his job as foreman at the Embry place. He'd initially taken the job for two reasons. First, he wanted to be near Laura. And second, Senator Sutton believed only his eldest son should inherit the Sutton lands. Chase understood his father's reasons and had made his plans accordingly. He'd hoped to marry Laura and eventually own the Embry ranch. But nothing had gone right. Laura was gone, accused of murdering his brother.

Her disappearance hadn't just affected him. The Embrys were devastated by Laura's apparent guilt. Chase wouldn't quit on them, too. So he had stayed as foreman, secure in the knowledge that the Senator didn't consider Chase's job an act of betrayal. Besides Chase didn't see how leaving the Embrys in the lurch would bring back Brent. The only thing he could do for his brother was seek justice. In spite of all Brent's shortcomings, he hadn't deserved to be murdered.

And Chase hadn't deserved to have his hopes for the future, of raising a family on the lands he loved, destroyed. He'd thought Laura had been as crazy about him as he was about her. He'd hoped to marry her and modernize the Embry ranch. Building a home with Laura had been all he ever wanted, but those dreams had died with Brent.

At the memories of what could have been, his stance hardened. His father might be powerful, wealthy and a take-charge kind of man, but he wouldn't break the law. "The Senator wouldn't tamper with evidence."

Laura shook her head. "He wouldn't have to. You know how everyone in Highview respects him. He's done favors for people going back twenty, thirty years. A man like your father will have automatic sympathy whether he asks for it or not. Once Brent Sutton's name is spoken any jury will be prejudiced in his favor. Plenty of judges, the district attorney, even the newspapers will automatically slant things in your father's favor.''

Chase stepped back, leaned against the cool brass wall of the elevator and crossed his arms over his chest. "You saying Brent's not entitled to justice?"

She drew herself up so straight, her back cracked. "*I'm* entitled to justice. And I would never get it— not in Highview. Not in Colorado."

His fists clenched and unclenched. This conversation wasn't going the way he'd planned. In every scenario he'd played out in his head, she was supposed to claim she was innocent. The disappointment of hearing the devastating truth from the lips he'd once adored threatened to tear him apart.

Chase fought down the nausea that rose in his throat, his expression betraying none of his inner turmoil. Cursing himself for a fool, he still needed to hear her say the words. "You're guilty, aren't you?"

"Yes."

As soon as she said it, he wanted her to take it back. Deny the truth. Lie. And he found the thought contemptible. Brent was his blood, his brother. They had grown up in the same house. They'd shared pony rides and chocolate chip cookies, traded baseball cards and girlie magazines.

Chase told himself he was a Sutton. And Suttons were loyal to their family, their land and their law. Suttons stuck together. As much as Chase wanted to, he couldn't make excuses for Laura Embry any longer.

Those treasured memories of holding her could no longer keep him warm at night. Now they were only a mockery of what he'd once thought possible.

By murdering his brother, she'd killed their love and any chance for a future together.

He should walk away. But he could not—not until she told him why. He couldn't go on with his life until he knew what had happened that night.

She had other ideas. She picked up her papers, then stabbed the Clear button with a shaking finger and the elevator rose smoothly. "This is neither the time nor the place to—"

"Why?"

"Because if we don't leave—" she gestured to the elevator with an unsteady hand "—the fire department will attempt a rescue."

She'd misunderstood him, but he let the elevator continue its upward movement. "Why'd you kill my brother?"

At his question, pain flickered in her eyes and she kept her voice unnaturally calm. "You're right, we need to talk. But I have to meet a client for a real estate closing."

"Put him off."

"I do title work. Without my presence, the real estate transaction won't close. It wouldn't be fair to the buyer, the seller or the real estate agents. Besides, I need the money. Let's meet—"

"For dinner?"

"At my apartment. I assume you have the address?"

He'd barely nodded before the elevator doors opened and she slipped by without waiting for his consent. "I'll expect you there at five."

Angered by her curt dismissal, he took her hand and held her back, surprised at the icy coolness of her flesh. "How do I know you won't run again?"

"You don't." Amid a crowd of curious office workers waiting for the elevator, she jerked free, her cheeks flushing.

He'd never before questioned her honesty. But that was before he knew she was a murderer. While she'd matured in the two years since he'd seen her last, she was harder around the edges, but he sensed a fragility in her core. As she walked away, he wondered if he wanted to hear her explanation, if he could bear to have her shatter any more of his illusions.

He'd delayed reporting her location to the authorities, wanting to hear her side first. Now he had a decision to make.

AT FIVE O'CLOCK sharp, Chase pulled into Laura's apartment complex, all pavement and concrete block, boasting a few scraggly palmettos beneath a lone granddaddy oak weeping with Spanish moss. Chase parked, adrenaline coursing through him. He wanted justice on several levels and his short talk with Laura in the elevator had proved unsatisfactory in more ways than one.

He still didn't know why she'd killed his brother. During her admission, her eyes had revealed such sharp pain that he would never forget it. And yet while he'd sensed her sorrow, he couldn't shake the feeling that *she* didn't think she'd done anything wrong. It wasn't what she'd said, so much as the proud tilt of her chin, shoulders squared in defiance and the straight backbone holding her erect that puzzled him.

Exposing her, even for justice, made his skin

crawl with disgust. He felt lower than a toad in a posthole for cornering her, accusing her.

But she had killed his brother.

All his feelings for her should have died with Brent. He didn't want to feel tender emotions for an admitted murderess, didn't want to find her attractive, didn't want to spend another sleepless night mourning what they'd lost. He didn't want to want her. Unfortunately, the shock of seeing her again had generated emotions he thought he'd put behind him.

Under the sweltering Louisiana sun, he strode across a narrow walkway and through a courtyard paved with cracked stones and decorated with wilted blue flowers, forcing himself to concentrate on his mission. The Senator had begun drumming loyalty to family into his sons long before they started school. The lesson took root and grew with the passing years. Chase wanted to do the right thing for the Suttons.

Yet Laura must have had good reason to commit such a violent act. No matter how much personal pain it cost him, dogged determination would make him see justice through to the end.

Chase glanced at his watch. Would she be here? Aggravated that he might meet Laura's husband set his impatient feet stepping with a speed he usually saved for a crisis.

He passed by a row of mail slots, looking for "Embry" until he recalled that she would no longer use her maiden name. Simmering with annoyance, he searched for her new, married name, the name she'd used when she'd written her parents a letter by way of an old high school friend, and that Chase had seen on her father's desk.

Slowly, methodically, he intended to break down the wall of lies she'd built to keep him away. And by tracking her down, he'd hoped to annoy her as much as she'd disturbed him. He knocked on her door and the wait seemed endless.

She eyed him through the peephole, then finally unchained and opened the door. "I was hoping you wouldn't show."

He'd been about to berate her for her lack of courtesy, but she looked so weary. Although she'd run from him for two years, he'd finally found her. He told himself he was a patient man and reined in his aggravation.

She'd changed out of work clothes into a T-shirt and jeans, reminding him of the woman he'd thought he'd known so well. Except this woman belonged to another man. She used his name and wore a wedding ring to prove it. He told himself the smudge on her cheek was none of his concern and hooked his fingers in his belt to prevent himself from smoothing away the dirt.

After locking the door behind them, she led him through a hallway, past cartons half-packed with linens and dishes into a living area lacking in furniture, except for a battered couch stacked with assorted kitchen paraphernalia and an old TV. That she'd intended to disappear again, he had no doubt.

No wonder she looked so tired. Picking up and starting a new life couldn't be easy. He imagined she'd lived the last two years looking over her shoulder, worried she'd make a mistake, fearful every day that she'd be caught.

But no matter how frazzled, how weary, how sorry she was, he couldn't let her run away from murder. And she was obviously getting ready to split again. Anger that she refused to face the consequences of her actions hardened his tone. "Going somewhere?"

"If you can find me, then so can the law."

"They didn't have the advantage I did."

She cocked an eyebrow. "Meaning?"

"I doubt they'll enter the Embry homestead and find your letters on your dad's desk."

Her jaw dropped and sadness filled her eyes. "He saved them?"

It was typical of her to think first of her family's love for her and not how her father's carelessness with her letters endangered her freedom. Memories of what she'd done to the family she loved turned his voice harsh. "What'd you expect? That's all they have of you now. Your mother's aged ten years. Your father never smiles."

"Stop it." Her voice rose and cracked. Slumping against the wall, she slid to the carpet, leaned her head back against the wall and closed her eyes. "You have no right to come here and—"

"*You* said we needed to talk. Was that simply an excuse to get rid of me until you disappeared again?"

She didn't open her eyes but rubbed her temple as if it throbbed, looking so fragile and vulnerable he had to remind himself what she'd done. His question hung in the air and the silence grew taut.

Finally she opened her eyes and spoke softly. "I meant what I said about us talking."

He gestured to the boxes. "Doesn't look like it."

"I'm scared, Chase. Scared I'll spend the rest of my life behind bars for—"

"Maybe you belong in jail."

She hugged her knees tightly, the gold band on her finger mocking him. "It was an accident."

He paced the carpet in front of her, resisted the urge to shake her for playing word games. "You said you killed him."

She picked at nonexistent lint on the frayed knee of her jeans. "That night, Brent was so drunk he had no more judgment than a raging bull. He wanted to brand Rafe's day-old foal. I thought if I could stall him long enough, you would show up and stop him."

"I delivered a calf that night. Brent was supposed to call. Let you know."

"He didn't."

"And?"

"When I showed at the barn, he was about to brand the foal."

Chase frowned, recalling the powerful and muscular animal with well-developed quarters, sloping shoulders and good depth in its chest that was Rafe's prize possession. "Rafe tattoos the inner lip. He doesn't ruin beautiful horseflesh."

"I thought I could talk Brent out of it. He was waving the hot brand like an implement from the Spanish Inquisition. Talking crazy." She looked at the rug, then back at him. "There was no reasoning with him. I kept praying you would come. When you didn't—"

"You grabbed up the pitchfork?"

"I thought Brent would back off. Instead he stumbled, fell forward and the tines…" She drew a deep breath. "It was an accident."

"That's the entire story?" He'd watched her eyes

carefully, and while she'd held his gaze through most of the telling, he suspected she was leaving something out. Something vital. Something she didn't want to admit.

As much as he wanted to give her the benefit of the doubt, he knew Laura might have had a reason to commit murder. The night Brent had died and Laura had disappeared, Chase had searched Laura's room, looking for a clue to where she might have fled. He couldn't miss the box in the bathroom trash, the pregnancy stick. He knew that the night she'd murdered Brent, she'd believed she was pregnant. With Chase's child? Or was it possible his brother had inadvertently walked into a lover's quarrel? Could Laura have had a second lover who had refused to marry her and Brent got in the middle of the fight?

Chase didn't believe it. Two weeks before that night, she'd come to him a virgin. Maybe he was looking for excuses for a murderer, but it wasn't Laura's nature to flirt or sleep with other men.

And yet, she still hadn't mentioned her condition. Could the pregnancy test have been false? Had she carried the baby to term? He'd always believed she'd been pregnant with *his* child.

She sat on the floor, twisting the gold band on her finger nervously. And he realized he didn't know this woman. He'd never have thought Laura Embry capable of defending herself with a pitchfork, of accidentally killing anyone—never mind his tall, powerful brother. The old Laura wouldn't have had the cunning to hide her identity and start a new life. Had the woman he thought he'd known so well changed?

Or had he never really known her at all? Maybe her new husband didn't know her any better.

"Is your husband aware of your past?" He didn't bother to hide the hurt and anger in his voice.

"There is no husband." She held up her ring finger. "This is just another lie to hide my real identity."

At her admission, tightness eased in his chest. But he wouldn't let himself dwell on her words or whether the child she'd carried had been his. He couldn't go there. Not now. Maybe not ever.

Instead he lowered himself to the carpet and faced her at eye level. "If you don't come back with me, your entire life will be a lie. Is that what you want?"

"Maybe that's what I deserve." She drew up her knees and rested her forehead against them.

"Is that what you think?"

"I don't want to think. I want to forget." Her mouth twisted with regret and distress. She took the ring off her finger and flung it against the wall. "Why can't you just go home and pretend you never found me?"

She'd lashed out like a wounded animal, but he couldn't let her pain affect him. "It's time for you to come home."

"Damn you. My home is here now. I've made a new life for myself."

"A good life?" He gestured to the bare walls, the half-packed boxes, the tacky kitchen linoleum. Two years ago, she'd been carefree, happy. She'd had loving parents, solid roots at the Embry ranch. Since then, she'd been damaged. Now, she seemed so alone. As he stared into her eyes, listened to her words, he caught a flash of her trapped soul. But nothing was clear except that she didn't welcome him back into her life—as if she accepted pain and loneliness worse than his.

The doorbell rang. Laura leapt to her feet as if betrayed, and he caught another glimpse of anguish in her voice as it turned chilly. "You called the cops?"

Gently, Chase touched her cheek and smoothed away the dust, regretting that he must hurt her even more. "I won't let you spend your life running."

Chapter Two

Laura slapped his hand from her cheek. If Chase had reported Laura to the law, she wanted no tender displays from him. "How dare you?"

She couldn't think when he touched her with such gentleness, his gesture bringing back memories of carefree days riding through green pastures, of nights of passion, of an untroubled life that she'd never know again.

As much as she missed the Embry ranch that had been her anchor in her old life, this new life—driftless at sea—was better than drowning in jail. But Chase's relentless pursuit had most likely led to those ominous knocks on the door and now, she'd probably be convicted of murder.

Chase shrugged as if touching her meant nothing. "You had a smudge of dirt. It's gone now."

"Great. You want me to look good for a mug shot?" Voice acerbic, she tensed, ready to bolt out the back door.

He read her intent to flee as easily as a stampeding herd and shackled her wrist in a firm grip. Experience and memories told her she couldn't fight hands callused and strong from stringing fences, shoulders corded with muscle from lifting hay bales, an iron will that couldn't be swayed by argument.

It took every ounce of will and pride not to struggle. Instead she squared her shoulders, faced his implacable stare. "Let go of me."

"It's time to stop running."

"That's my decision."

"Is it?" Chase's gray eyes darkened with challenge. His chin jutted with a stubbornness she'd once found comforting. But there was nothing comforting about him now. A muscle in his jaw throbbed with unleashed tension and the fire in his eyes threatened to burn her to cinders. "What you do next is a decision *we* make together."

His hold on her wrist said otherwise. His hold told her she'd run out of choices.

Her actions had trapped her in a nightmare. A nightmare of lying to everyone she met. Fearful someone would recognize her. Worried over what she had done to those she'd loved most. The pain she'd caused her parents made her weep. The pain she'd caused Chase she'd buried so deep because whenever she let it surface, it threatened to destroy her.

The knocks on the door started again, louder, more urgent.

No matter how futile she knew her words would be, she couldn't let him put a noose around her neck and lead her to slaughter—at least not without a fight.

"Don't you get it?" Her voice shook. "No one will believe Brent's death was an accident. I'll spend the rest of my life in jail."

At her angry words, he increased the pressure on

her wrist. Not enough to hurt—just enough to trap her and drag her toward the door. "You're being paranoid. You're wrong."

She shook her head. "Don't you think I wanted to go to you that night? Tell you what happened?"

"You didn't."

"I knew you'd believe the justice system would be fair. I didn't."

"I won't let you live like this—afraid of a knock on the door."

"How I live is not up to you. That's my decision."

Nothing she'd said had changed his mind. Chase continued his advance to the door and even before he spoke she knew he wouldn't let her go. He was a man of deep convictions, immeasurable grit and stubborn stamina. If he was a different kind of man, she might convince him to give up, go home. But Chase didn't have the word *quit* in his vocabulary. He took pride in completing every task, each project, with a stubborn attention to detail. Intense, single-minded effort came to him as naturally as busting broncos. And this task he'd set himself, of finding her, turning her in to the law so his brother would receive justice could be no different—he would see it through.

His fingers, hot and tough, shackled her to his side. "So we'll agree to disagree."

"This isn't a silly argument where compromise solves the problem. That's why I ran from Colorado." That and the fact that if she hadn't stopped Brent from raping her, she might have lost the child she'd been carrying. Chase's son. The son he didn't know he had.

As much as she'd missed Chase, she'd dreaded seeing him again with every cell in her being. She'd protected his unborn child from Brent's lust and she'd made sure the child wasn't born in prison. But knowing what she had done to Chase was unbearable. Putting him between his family and her, dividing his loyalties could tear a square shooter like him in two.

The knock grew more insistent.

If he answered that door, she'd spend the rest of her life in jail. Blood roared in her ears like waves pounding against a rocky shore. She'd already lost Chase and she couldn't bear to lose her son, too.

With firm logic, she tried to calm the icy panic. As much as Keith needed his mother, she'd tried to prepare him for this moment. And yet, at just the thought of never seeing her baby again, she swallowed back tears.

Despite her best intentions, she jerked her hand in an attempt to free herself. "Damn you. Don't turn me in."

"Is that what you think I'm doing?"

She couldn't fight his brawn. The moment she'd dreaded for two years upended her steadiness like quicksand beneath her feet. Her legs wouldn't work, knees dissolving to jelly and the bitter nausea in her stomach churned.

"Don't open the door," she pleaded. Ignoring her entreaty, he kept her imprisoned, unlocked the dead bolt.

For a moment, Chase's massive shoulders hid the view. She imagined uniformed officers, handcuffs, the humiliation of Chase thrusting her into their custody.

Peeking around him, she saw her neighbor at the door. No police to cart her to jail. Just her neighbor in her crisp white nurse's uniform, holding a sleeping fifteen-month-old in her arms. But Laura had no time to feel relief or dwell on how paranoid she'd become by thinking Chase had called the cops when he didn't.

Chase was studying her son, hard speculation in his eyes. He focused on the boy, lips drawn tight in intense deliberation while Laura held her breath, waiting for Chase to comment on the baby's dark coloring, black hair and stubborn chin and how much her baby looked like a miniature Sutton. But Chase said nothing, staring fascinated, fiercely, ferociously.

And somehow as though knowing with her son right there she wouldn't flee, he released her wrist.

As if sensing she'd interrupted an awkward situation, her neighbor flushed. "I'm sorry. I told you I'd watch Keith, but the hospital called me in to work. A pileup in the French Quarter. The choppers are airlifting the injured right now. I have to go." She thrust the sleeping boy into Laura's arms, then hesitated, looking from Chase to the child and opening her mouth to comment.

Laura caught her neighbor's eye and shook her head. "Thanks for watching him for me."

She hugged the baby to her chest and without daring to look at Chase, carried Keith into his room. Chase followed her every step but remained eerily silent, staring at the crib, the baby pictures on the wall, the few toys she had still to pack. Was he trying to figure out the dates? Why didn't he say something?

As she covered Keith with a blanket and smoothed back his hair and breathed in the scent of baby oil and corn starch, she realized she dreaded telling Chase about his son. She preferred to go on thinking of herself as the sole parent, the caretaker Keith needed. With Chase fully capable of assuming parental responsibilities, she became unnecessary. She could no longer tell herself she'd avoided the law in order to take care of her son.

Swallowing hard, she left the baby to sleep, wondering if she could convince Chase to leave them to live their own lives. She ached to watch her son speak his first sentence, learn to read and ride, and grow into a man. One look at Chase's chiseled face and she knew she'd stolen all the time she could. Lips grim, eyes narrowed, he drew his brow into a fierce scowl. She could almost hear his teeth gnashing.

Somehow, somewhere she would find the strength to face him.

"HOW ABOUT SOME iced tea?" Laura offered Chase, more to have something to do than to quench any thirst.

Chase followed her into the kitchen and pulled up a stool at the eat-in bar. "Sure."

She took a pitcher out of the fridge, filled a glass with ice and poured. He sipped the tea and swiveled on the bar stool as she returned to packing.

It seemed peculiar to have him sitting in her kitchen and she knew they were simply delaying the discussion. But for just a minute, it felt good to let the tension ease from her shoulders and pretend that the intervening two years had never happened. Back on the Embry spread, she'd often made Chase big sandwiches, which he downed with cold milk.

And she'd taken a primitive pleasure in watching him consume vast quantities of food. She liked watching his white teeth bite into a meal she'd prepared. He'd share stories of roping and riding or his concerns about the stock while she told him about her classes at the community college. She'd been so much younger then with a bright future ahead of her.

She'd liked the idea of staking her claim to the middle Sutton son. While the Senator had saddled his eldest son Brent with the responsibility of running the entire ranch, he'd encouraged his other sons to find different paths to success. Chase had been foreman at the Embry ranch for years, an arrangement that suited her parents who needed steady and competent help but which also kept Chase close to his family yet free to spend his spare hours with Laura.

Sundays, Chase ate dinner with his influential father and his affectionately rowdy brothers. Laura had often accompanied him, enjoying the way the four brothers teased one another, yet surprised at the boisterous discussions among them. Because outside the home, the boys stuck together, a wall of family solidarity.

The Senator treasured his large family, developing their sense of loyalty and family pride. He had presided over the dinner table with quiet dignity, cognizant of and comfortable with his power and strength, yet he'd never lost touch with his roots. In Colorado, the Senator had attained legendary status, helping out ranchers in need, fighting for more money for agricultural education, representing their concerns in Washington.

While the Senator trained Brent, the eldest and heir apparent, to take over the largest ranch in the state, he encouraged his four younger sons to seek other careers with a savvy that Laura had found as ambitious as his political aspirations. There were rumors the powerful Senator might make it to the White House. While Laura would vote for him, she was in awe of him, too, and had been glad he seemed to approve of her relationship with his son.

But she'd also been thankful Chase had had no interest in politics. He wanted to ranch. And Highview was all the home she'd ever wanted.

The Embry spread might not have the wealth that marked the Sutton Ranch, or boast five sons to run it, but as an only child, Laura had been spoiled with loving attention from both parents. While she'd often wished for a brother or sister, her parents had hired help with children around her age so she never lacked for playmates. Busy and content, she'd been a teenager before she realized that not every marriage was as happy as her parents'. Her father still looked at her mother with a sparkle in his eyes. The same way Chase had once looked at her.

In turn, she'd adored Chase. He didn't flit from girl to girl. He took his responsibilities seriously, yet he knew how to show her a good time, too. Most of all, she'd liked the way he'd made her feel—as if she were the most special person in the world.

But those were the feelings of an innocent girl and seemed a lifetime ago. Laura was no longer innocent. How could she be after committing murder?

She folded a blanket and placed it in the open

packing box on the sofa and stole a sideways glance at Chase as he drank his tea. He, too, had changed. He appeared more self-contained. His easy smile had been replaced with a stoic rigidity that made it difficult for her to tell his thoughts. And he said little. She remembered him as more talkative. She couldn't believe he hadn't questioned her about Keith. Couldn't he see the child had his eyes, his hair, his coloring?

While she wrapped kitchen utensils in newspaper, Chase rested his elbows on the counter. "If you remain on the run, you can't give your son the kind of future he needs."

Apparently, he had yet to go to the law. She still had time to persuade him. However, the man was as stubborn as a mule. He would keep pressing, wear her down. But she'd fought too hard for her freedom to stop now. "I can't give Keith any kind of future from a jail cell."

Her rush of defiance seemed to fuel his anger. Chase slapped his palm on the counter. "Damn it! Think of your son. Will you give him fake names to remember? Move from place to place so the boy has no roots, no friends, no family? Have your folks even seen their grandchild?"

She shook her head and chewed her bottom lip, knowing he deserved answers, knowing Keith deserved more than a life on the run, wondering if she had been selfish. She also wondered why Chase hadn't yet asked if Keith was his son. Chase could count backwards as well as any man, but maybe he wasn't yet ready to face more pain. She'd kept father from son, a crime he'd consider as much a betrayal a murder. Chase didn't deserve her lies. And she could do better by her son. If she kept hiding, she would condemn her son to her life-style.

She'd been so busy surviving, she hadn't thought enough about the future. It had taken all her energy to concoct a new identity and land a job at the title insurance agency. Leave it to Chase to take one look at her baby and start planning five, ten and twenty years down the road.

While Keith had been an infant, he'd needed her. But soon he would wonder why he didn't have a father, or grandparents. More importantly, he'd never have the security of setting roots into the land or of having a home. Was it fair to deny him the pleasure of playing in green pastures, of learning the cycles of nature, of being one with the land? If she hid from her past, she'd be depriving him of family, a way of life that was his heritage. But if she went home, she'd deprive him of a mother.

She placed the glasses in the carton on top of the folded blanket. Enough was enough. "Don't you think I want him to meet his grandparents?"

"Come back with me."

She looked up to see Chase leaning close. Too close. She could see a light stubble darkening the hollows of his cheeks and chin...and anger smoking in his gray eyes.

"It's too big a risk."

Chase used the same coaxing tone on her that he used on skittish horses. "Keith deserves a better life than you can give him here."

"I'm a good mother." Even as she protested, a lump clogged her throat. She couldn't meet Chase's gaze. Instead she concentrated on packing more paper between the glasses and plates as if her life depended on it.

"A good mother would put her son's future before her own."

His savage words struck her like a slap across the face. In another man, the suppressed violence in his statement might have frightened her. In Chase, the fierce emotions blazing in his eyes revealed frustration and sorrow and loyalty to a brother who had died.

And while she could admire his loyalty to the Suttons, it reminded her how much she loved her own family. She wanted the best life possible for her son—even if she had to give him up. Her folks would see to Keith. He'd grow up on the ranch, enjoy a stable home, loving grandparents. And Chase would be a terrific father once she told him the truth.

She owed it to her son to find the courage to try to clear her name of murder—even if it meant taking the risk of spending the rest of her life in jail.

Chase reached over the box, removed the sugar bowl from her hand, his warm fingers steadying her. His thumb rubbed a gentle circle at her wrist.

"I've made reservations on the nine o'clock flight." He reached into his shirt pocket and tapped the airline tickets on the box. "We'll do this together—for Keith's sake."

Chase's silence on the question of Keith's paternity had her as nervous as a long-tailed cat under a rocking chair. He'd always known how to get to her. She might have let him win the argument but she wouldn't accept the pity in his eyes. Snatching back her hand, she shoved the sugar bowl in with the rest of her things. "First, I need to finish packing."

"IT'S GOOD TO have you home." Laura's mother handed her a cup of coffee and pushed the cream her way. Anna Embry, tall like her daughter, had aged with a natural grace. In the morning light, Laura could see that her blond hair was now streaked with gray, her round face creased with wrinkles, her lips curled up in a contented smile that she remembered so well. Anna rested her hand on Laura's shoulder and squeezed, seemingly unable to resist touching her only child.

"It's good to be home." Laura took comfort in the blue Colorado skies, the solidity of the hovering mountains and her mother's warmth. Home. She hadn't realized how much she'd missed the quiet, the serene pastures and the crisp, dry air until she'd returned last night with Chase and Keith.

She'd grown up in the house that seemed to sprout right out of the earth, as permanent and substantial and sure as the land, the grass and the Rocky Mountains. Her eyes eagerly took in the massive stone fireplace that dominated the combination living and kitchen area. She let herself enjoy the two-tone shag carpeting that had faded since she'd been gone, but the wood paneling on the wall full of pictures and her dad's rodeo trophies remained just as she remembered. Cattle industry publications covered a coffee table in front of a massive sofa. She recalled frigid winter nights there, snuggled under a blanket, a cup of hot cocoa beside her while her mother crocheted and her father read to them. On the kitchen windowsill, Anna still kept her grand-

mother's pitcher, the one her mother used to fill with
the wildflowers Laura would gather on picnic out-
ings. As the scent of lemon-waxed parquet floors,
coffee and chicken-fried steak smothered in thick
cream gravy welcomed her, Laura's tensions had
eased.

The family reunion last night had been joyful, but
not bittersweet, each of them holding raw emotions
in check. Her folks had always been there for her
and she couldn't have been more grateful. There had
been no words of recrimination, only acceptance and
discussion of the difficulties ahead.

This morning, her mother's blue eyes, so much
like her own, hid her doubts and questions with a
determinedly cheerful demeanor. Her calming influ-
ence helped steady Laura's nerves and her dull ache
of foreboding.

Across the table, her father casually turned the
page of his newspaper as though today were ordi-
nary. "Thought I'd take the boy for a ride."

Usually her father would be at work at least an
hour before dawn, but he'd stayed inside today, his
presence alone showing how much he'd missed her.
His words might be gruff but he wasn't fooling anyone. She'd seen him peek into Keith's room three
times already, unable to contain his eagerness for
his grandson to awaken.

"Dad, Keith's just learned to walk three months
ago."

"I had you riding before you cut your first tooth."

Laura sipped her coffee, unable to eat Anna's
homemade flapjacks, afraid they'd stick in her
throat. "That was a long time ago."

Anna placed a plate of crisp bacon and some maple syrup on the table. "Seems like yesterday to me. I remember you at Keith's age. You'd sneak out of bed still in your pajamas and toddle off with your dad to help him do chores."

Her father chuckled. "And then they'd take twice as long."

Anna watched Laura play with her food but didn't urge her to eat. Her mother knew her so well, knew she was edgy about talking to the attorney, then turning herself in to the sheriff and hoping to make bail. This might be the last meal the three of them ever shared.

At least, whatever happened, Keith would be in loving hands.

A truck purred into the front yard, drowning out George Strait on the radio. Laura looked up to see Chase sipping from his coffee mug as he came up the steps, wearing jeans snug enough to stop her circulation.

He knocked and entered with a pantherlike grace and a comfort level that revealed how much time he spent at the Embry ranch. He tipped his hat to her folks. "Morning."

Anna rose to her feet and gave him a hug. "How about some flapjacks?"

"No, thanks." He held up a coffee mug and a lock of dark hair fell over his eyes giving him a rakish look. "I could use a refill."

Normal conversation usually focused on cows, horses, grass, rain and land. And which cowboy was fixing to doctor a sick calf, placing orders for feed, stringing fences or moving cattle from one pasture to another. She hadn't heard mention of Chase's favorites—embryo transfers and genetics—in two long years. Other things were on all their minds. Like how things would go with the attorney they'd called yesterday and whom they were about to go meet.

Chase eyed her over the brim of his cup. "You ready?"

"Yes." *No.* Wrapped in a cocoon of anguish, Laura shoved back her chair, her thoughts murkier than her coffee dregs. "I want to say goodbye to Keith."

Anna had his room ready when they'd arrived last night. Of necessity, letters between them had been rare, but within a week of Keith's birth, her parents had known they had a grandson. Laura suspected her mother had had the room ready for over a year. The bright animal-printed wallpaper matched the characters painted on the side of the crib. A hand-carved rocking horse with a miniature leather saddle stood in the corner.

Keith reclined on his side, peaceful in sleep while her heart tumbled down a steep mountain, bruising with every bounce. She had no intention of waking him but smoothed his baby-fine hair with a palm, sneaked one last kiss to his brow and breathed in his baby-soft scent.

Tears, as sharp as iron filings, sliced her throat. Unable to resist holding him, she scooped Keith into her arms. He wakened immediately, dark eyes opening with enthusiastic curiosity at his new surroundings.

"Hi, sweetie. You're going to like living here." She kept her voice cheerful but her feet felt tethered and she forced them across the room to the changing table with uncharacteristic slowness.

"Down." Already fixing to explore his new surroundings, Keith wriggled in her arms.

After changing his diaper, she longed to scoop him back up. Instead she let him have his wish and took pleasure in watching him toddle toward the sounds of activity in the kitchen.

"Eat. Eat. Eat."

She heard the newspaper flutter to the floor and her dad's gruff tone softened. "Come here, you big ol' boy."

"Me, big," Keith agreed, proudly.

Laura stood paralyzed, unable to enter the kitchen. A shudder ripped through her and she fought it, bent on regaining control of shattering sadness. Unable to sleep last night and with the time change throwing her natural clock out of rhythm, she was weary, wearier than she'd ever been. Had it only been her life in the balance, she could have dealt with the consequences. But with the knowledge of what her parents would have to bear, the exhaustion suddenly seemed too much and her mind clouded with anxiety.

At least they would have Keith. The baby would help them to look to the future. But what would happen when she told Chase that he was her baby's father? She owed Chase that much. And she knew him well enough to realize he would insist on raising his son.

It was her fault that her parents might lose both their child and grandchild in one giant mess. Laura resisted the urge to run into her room and hide under her covers. She'd spent enough time hiding. No more. She might as well accept her fate. Only why did that include hurting every person she had ever loved?

In shadow, she leaned against the wall, suddenly realizing that from his angle, Chase could see her. His gaze drilled her, showing no signs of relenting and she bit her lip to stifle a moan. Layered with stubborn determination and innate compassion, his vitality strengthened her, infusing her with an energy to go on.

Inch by inch, she forced feeling back into her fingers and toes, her hands and feet, her arms and legs. Pride kept her upright, walking like a robot, and spine erect, she forced her feet toward the kitchen.

Her mother hugged her goodbye, a tear escaping down one cheek. Her father waved while bouncing Keith on his knee, but she noted his Adam's apple bob as he swallowed hard.

All too soon, she found herself alone with Chase in the truck. The brilliant sunlight and bright blue sky mocked the shadow hovering over her. Despite the day's warmth, she shivered in foreboding. With town only half an hour away, she wet her lips and prayed for courage to talk to Chase about the son that he surely knew was his.

Chapter Three

After a restless night watching the Embry house to make sure Laura didn't leave, Chase's thoughts were spinning round. Earlier this morning, his brother Tyler had spelled Chase long enough to shower, shave and change clothes.

Two inches taller than Chase but leaner, Tyler stirred his share of attention from the ladies, who took to him like a bear to a honey tree. Now that he was the heir apparent, he probably didn't have time to date. Maybe he was better off. He took his responsibilities seriously, but Chase didn't envy him the enormous task of running the huge Sutton spread.

And yet Chase took comfort and pride in knowing that Suttons would always own land in Colorado. Chase might foreman the Embry ranch down the road but he could return to visit his brothers, fish the wide rivers and ride through mile upon mile of cattle land. Someday he would teach his children to appreciate the sweeping vistas of the Sutton Ranch and to savor the respect and devotion that the Suttons had for family.

Suttons stuck together. Because Chase had

tracked Laura down and there could soon be a trial, his brother Cameron was flying back from Boston. Last night Rafe had called from Texas where he was trying to buy a mare, asking if he could do anything to help, telling Chase not to do anything Rafe wouldn't do. When Chase had snorted and asked slick-tongued Rafe exactly what *he* wouldn't do, for once, Rafe hadn't had an answer. And Tyler had taken his valuable time away from running the Sutton spread to help Chase make sure Laura didn't decide to leave during the night.

When Chase had returned to the stakeout just before dawn, Tyler handed him a sandwich and a thermos of coffee. "You want me to tell the Senator you're back?"

"He's in town?"

"Yep."

More shaken than he wanted to admit, Chase appreciated the information, knowing it couldn't alter his plans. He swung into the driver's side of his truck. "I was fixing to talk to him myself."

Tyler lightly punched his shoulder. "I know you haven't been studying to be a half-wit—"

"Careful." With a casual tap and an affectionate curl of his lip, Chase knocked his brother's hat down over his eyes. "I want to drink this coffee in peace."

Tyler pushed his hat back with his thumb and eyed Chase with an expression far wiser than his years. His hand fiddled with the armrest and he shifted in the truck's seat. Clearly uncomfortable, Tyler didn't want to delve into the topic on both their minds. But Suttons didn't avoid the hard stuff. They stopped stampedes, rode bucking broncos and shared their feelings when necessary.

Tyler gazed at Chase with a steady determination and spoke, keeping his drawl even. "Don't you be thinking there's nothing under my hat but hair. You coming back here with *her*—how's that going to look to the Senator?"

Chase didn't want to go there, either. He wanted to be alone with his thoughts, but Tyler could be more persistent than a hungry mosquito and the Senator meant too much to him to ignore his father's opinion. "How does my bringing her back here look to you?"

Tyler shook his head, one eyebrow cocked with incredulity, as if he couldn't believe that a Sutton brother would have the gall to ask him that. Shooting Chase with a troubled stare, Tyler let his doubt pierce through. "Whose side are you on?"

Chase supposed he should have expected the question and the edge of suspicion that came with it. He'd been so caught up in dealing with his own problems, he hadn't thought everything through. His brother deserved an answer. Only Chase didn't have one.

He sipped his coffee and through the windshield watched the first rays of sun rippling over the mountains, wishing the peaceful night wouldn't end. He liked listening to the uncomplicated crickets chirp, liked the simple scent of dew-laden grass, liked the plain landscape where a man could see to the horizon without the complexity of civilization disfiguring the natural lay of the land.

Tyler nudged him and finally, Chase drew his scattered and unsettled thoughts together. "Do I have to pick a side?"

Letting loose a long, low whistle, Tyler popped

open the door. "Not choosing—*is* a decision. And your public show of disloyalty will rip the Senator's guts. Don't you think he's been through enough?"

"Damn it! Don't boil and roast me in guilt. Brent had a temper, especially when he'd been drinking. He must have made a few enemies. Dad knows I've been searching for—"

"—Brent's killer?"

"Justice." Chase worked a kink out of his neck, his heart lurching. "The Senator lets a man make up his own mind."

"I noticed."

"He respects my judgment," Chase stated, wondering who he was trying to convince.

"He always did make us think for ourselves," Tyler agreed with a nod, the jerky action betraying his opinion of Chase's decision. "I reckon he'll let you make your own mistakes, too."

Chase raised his cup to Tyler in a silent salute. "Thanks for the coffee and the company."

His brother took the hint, departing without another word, but not before squeezing Chase's shoulder with a show of affection. It was a Sutton gesture through and through, his way of acknowledging a damnable situation and of supporting his brother—even while implying he was wrong.

Ten minutes later, Chase gunned the engine and had driven over the rise to the Embry house. And now Laura sat beside him in his truck, every muscle tense as a jackrabbit ready to bolt. Mixed with pain, there was a toughness about her face and the smooth skin over high cheekbones steamed with too little color and resignation. Her eyes, the hue of a hot blue flame, simmered with maturity that hadn't been there before.

She remained quiet, stewing, and when he reached the spot where the dirt road of the Embry ranch merged with asphalt, he broke the silence. "You going to spit it out?"

"What?"

"Whatever you're fixing to tell me." His eyes flickered from the rearview mirror to her.

A bittersweet smile curled up her mouth. "Can you read my mind?"

"You were chewing your bottom lip."

Her smile disappeared. "Maybe you should pull over."

Without hesitation he did as she asked, stopping on the shoulder, then driving into a dense stand of pine. Too tense to sit, she exited the vehicle and headed for the trickling stream that paralleled the road.

He came up behind her and put his arms around her. She was startled for a moment but relaxed, nestling against his chest. The top of her head came to his chin and the scent of her shampoo wafted to him on the breeze. With her back to him, he held her, the contact causing waves of memories he preferred to forget to surge through him. A feather-tipped touch behind his ear. Girlish laughter. A bareback race through a cow pasture. A swim in moonlight. She'd once been so open with him, playful and carefree. Now, she guarded her words as carefully as a politician.

"There's no way to ease into the subject."

"Just tell me."

Her voice dropped to almost a whisper. "It's going to hurt."

"Tell me."

"What I've done to you isn't fair."

He placed his hands on her shoulders and turned her around until she faced him. Pain shadowed her eyes and his stomach clenched as if in anticipation of a blow. "You've got to trust me. Keith is my son, isn't he?"

"Yes."

Yes. He refrained from pumping his fist in the air in glorious victory. Instead, he gathered her close, holding her, taking comfort in the palpitation of her heart against his chest. He'd suspected from the moment he'd seen the boy—but looks could be deceiving. Keith had the Sutton dark hair, dark eyes and a mischievous smile that reminded him of Rafe, a charm that could have been Cameron's and the Senator's enthusiasm. He'd wanted so much for the baby to be his, he hadn't let himself dwell on it for fear of his thoughts becoming an obsession. And Laura had given him plenty of other distractions.

He had a son. A boy. A beautiful, healthy child. A wave of euphoria crashed over him and he tread misty-eyed in a sea of joyful thankfulness. He and Laura had a child, the first Sutton grandchild. But the bubbles of happiness soon popped at the grim reality of their situation—the mother of his son had murdered his brother.

He looked down into Laura's shimmering eyes that brimmed with unshed tears and wondered if he could ever forgive her for what she'd done to his family. She must have read the doubts in his eyes because she winced.

But to give her credit, she held his gaze. "If it means anything to you, I'm sorry." She let out a shuddering sigh. "But no matter what happens between us, no matter if I go to jail, for Keith's sake, we have to plan for his future."

"I want my son." The words came from his mouth without thinking, came from deep in his core, a blazing sense of rightness that he and the boy belonged together. Keith was a Sutton. He was family. Blood. And Suttons took care of their own.

"My folks will keep him if I don't make bail. Keith will be happy there. They—"

"Can't keep him from me."

Her eyes narrowed. "Do you think they would?"

"You did."

At his harsh accusation all color left her face as if he'd struck her with his fist. As he realized it was the truth of his words that hurt her, he damned himself for his carelessness. She was most likely going to jail. She was giving up their child. Trying to do the right thing.

But he hurt too, damn it. He should have been there when his son was born. Hell, he should have had nine months to pamper Laura while he looked forward to Keith's arrival. And she shouldn't have had to go through so much alone.

As if fearing he'd lash out at her again, Laura took a step backward. Her low heel caught in the pine needles and she stumbled. Automatically, he caught her elbow, but she jerked from his touch. The words trickled from her mouth, then picked up speed. "I didn't mean to hurt you. I didn't mean to hurt my parents. Or Keith. Or your family. I didn't even mean to hurt Brent."

He had no answer for her. While he ached to pull her against him and tell her everything would be fine, he couldn't move past what she had done. And she knew it. He read the knowledge in her eyes, recognized her defeat and her weariness as the realization set in that he couldn't forgive her. The implications pounded him like a jackhammer. His son would grow up knowing his mother had murdered his uncle. The press would have a field day. The Senator must be told.

No matter what happened, Chase was determined his son would know both his parents. Chase knew what it was like growing up without a parent. His mother had died of a heart attack when he was just a child and he still missed her. Chase wouldn't let his son grow up without Laura—not if he could help it.

Reaching into his pocket, he took out his cell phone. Laura made no move to stop him. Eyes raw with pain, she lifted her chin and squared her shoulders. "You asked me to trust you. Maybe I should have done that a long time ago. Instead, I ran. But I'm trusting you now. Call whomever you like. Do what you think best."

He refused to let her words tear his heart to tiny pieces. He had multiple obligations here—to his father, to himself and to his son. He had to be strong and he needed to make a decision. Because time was running out. Chase could think of no one better equipped to help him than the Senator. Laura's attorney was waiting in town, waiting to turn her over to the sheriff.

LAURA DIDN'T KNOW who Chase was calling on his phone. Maybe he no longer wanted to be seen with her and would ask the sheriff to come out here and collect her. At the moment she was too numb to care. When she told him about Keith, she'd watched Chase's eyes turn from joy to horror, his agony slashing away her last hope that he could ever forgive her.

Seeing the suffering she'd inflicted on Chase had shattered her. What good was the truth when all it brought was pain? But she'd had to tell him. Especially now that she couldn't be there for her son, Keith needed his father.

Chase spoke into his phone, his voice harsh, his eyes frigid. "Meet us at Mark Bradley's office."

Bradley was Highview's only trial attorney. She'd phoned him yesterday and he'd agreed to take her case, help her through the difficult process of turning herself in to the sheriff.

Chase and Laura didn't speak during the ride into town. From the muscle ticking in his jaw, to the hard line of his chin, he radiated fury like a volcano about to explode. Protecting what little self-confidence she had left, she'd pulled herself into an emotional shell, unable to look at him, unable to shoulder any more guilt and pain.

The road ran level, curved and dipped a little before emerging into Highview. The bustling town boasted a movie theater, a grocery store, a post office and a new Walmart surrounded by perhaps fifty other mostly flourishing businesses. Tourists flocked here during the summer months, stayed in the Highview Hotel, using the picturesque town as a base to go river rafting, hiking and fishing.

The courthouse, dazzlingly white where the morning sun touched it, stood tall. Beside it, Bradley's office nestled in the shadows, sharing the block with the local jail and Mell's Restaurant.

From Chase's icy demeanor, she expected him to drop her off and leave, anxious to be rid of her. But he walked around the truck and held the door open for her. With coldness radiating from him like icicles, he remained as frigid as mountain runoff, as aloof as snow.

Her feet froze to the floor, but jerkily she made them move. Concentrating, she put one foot in front of the other and entered Bradley's office, barely aware that Chase followed.

Loud voices stampeded from the back room, invading the staid waiting room. At the sight of Chase, Bradley's secretary Sally Walker, whom Laura recognized from high school, dropped her paperback to the desk, her face startled and guilty. Laura supposed the secretary should consider herself lucky that her boss hadn't caught her loafing on the job. Recollecting her professional demeanor quickly, Sally hastened to straighten several letters on her desk. The dark-haired woman gave Laura a cool nod, then focused on Chase with appreciation, her tone conveying her approval. "Good morning, Mr. Sutton."

Laura didn't take offense. A woman would have to have both feet in the grave not to notice Chase's good looks. Chase didn't even seem to notice the woman's friendly overture.

A loud voice from the back office prevented Sally from saying more. "Judge, I'm telling you, if the Senator's bill passes, it'll hurt us where it counts—in our pockets."

"Unfortunately, the public adores him. They don't know what he's really like," Bradley answered the irate voice in a mild tone and Laura suspected it was Judge Stewart in Bradley's office. Years back, the two lawyers had been partners until Stewart had won his seat on the bench. "People have a notion most attorneys are greedy vultures, and the Senator's feeding them more lies by exaggerating our income," Bradley continued in a persuasive tone.

"We need someone to tell our side." Judge Stewart's pitch grew deeper, more adamant. "The Senator has no right to legislate attorney fees. What's this country coming to? A man has to—"

"Mr. Sutton and Laura Embry are here to see you, sir." Sally spoke into her speaker phone, seemingly enjoying the fact that Chase had heard the men criticizing his father. But heck, that the judge and the Senator had differing political views was old news.

Judge Stewart must have exited out a side door because when Bradley ushered Chase and her into his office, there was no sign of anyone else. Bradley, a hefty man with a round face, gray hair and kindly green eyes had lived in Highview all his life, except for a short time when he'd gone away to law school in Texas. He knew most everyone and despite his earlier words about people not liking attorneys, juries believed in him.

Bradley offered them coffee which they both refused, then settled behind his desk. "Laura, after your phone call yesterday, I started my research, but I still need to hear the story in your own words."

His frank gaze moved to Chase who'd settled in a nearby chair. "We should be alone."

Chase met her gaze, his dark, thick lashes still. She studied him for a long moment, wishing she could heal the ugly wounds between them, knowing the scars ran too deep. But Chase had been with her from the beginning and he had earned the right to see this through to the end.

"I want him here," Laura countered. She'd told Chase she trusted him and she would keep her word.

Bradley picked up a pen and tapped it against a tablet. "As your attorney, I must advise you that your best interests…may not coincide with his."

The intercom crackled and Sally interrupted again. "The Senator and Tyler insist on seeing—"

An opening door drowned out the rest of her words. Senator Sutton and Tyler strode in and the room suddenly shrank. The Senator, tall and proud, with shoulders as wide as the Rockies nodded to Chase and she recalled once again how the Sutton men stood together. Now she knew whom Chase had called. His father.

If she hadn't been sitting, her knees would have buckled. She didn't know how to face the man that almost everyone in town liked. The Senator had a commanding presence—not so much from his sheer height but from the force of his intense personality. He expected people to act up to his expectations and most folks gave him their best efforts. To give him his due, he'd never lost his ability to make the locals feel like he was one of them.

Laura couldn't face him. She'd killed his son and borne his first grandchild. Despite the sickening swoop in her stomach, her sympathy for this proud man threatened to devastate her.

Tyler's appearance just added more Sutton testosterone to the room. Shorter than Chase and the Senator but still well over six feet, Tyler's face had acquired a toughness over the last two years. Whether it was Brent's murder or his new responsibilities that made him appear more mature, she couldn't say. But he'd clearly become a man in his own right.

Bradley leapt to his feet and pointed a finger at the Senator. "Damn it. You have no right to barge into my office. If you want an appointment, set a time with my secretary." His gaze flicked to the gun in Tyler's holster. "I won't condone violence here."

"No need to worry." Tyler folded his arms over his chest in a menacing gesture.

Chase rose to his feet, shook his father's hand and the two men exchanged a long look. "Thanks for coming."

"You asked him here?" Laura's voice rose in shock and confusion. Chase's move seemed the ultimate betrayal and yet she couldn't miss the tension between father and son.

Chase turned to her and knelt until his eyes were level with hers. "He should hear your story."

The intensity of Chase's look almost hypnotized her. He was willing her to agree, looking so deep into her, she couldn't break her gaze free. And all the while, her nerves scooted and skipped with restless anxiety. Should she do as he wanted?

If the Senator heard her story, he could go straight to the district attorney. But her deposition would give them the same information so she could see no legal advantage to Chase's maneuvering. But why had he invited the Senator to come? Why did he wish to cause his father more pain?

Bradley shook his head. "Absolutely not. Senator, please see yourself out and take Tyler with you."

Laura took a deep breath, her choice made. "Is it my decision?"

"Yes, but—"

"Then they stay."

A measure of respect caused Chase's pupils to darken and he exchanged a long, tense look with the Senator.

Bradley sputtered. "But—"

"What difference does it make?" the Senator asked with a reasonableness that hid the stress he must be under but still conveyed his disapproval. "I'll hear her now, and again at the trial."

"Anyone else you want to invite?" Bradley asked, acknowledging defeat as he settled back behind his desk.

"There's no need to make this harder," Chase chastised the attorney.

Laura steeled herself, praying to find the right words, reaching deep for the courage to get through the hellish story. The Senator stood, back against the wall, arms folded over his chest, a closed expression on his tanned and hardened features. Tyler paced until Chase glared at him and then both brothers pulled up chairs.

Bradley took out a tape recorder, set it on his desk and hit the play button. "Start at the beginning. Take your time."

Laura's mouth went dry but she forced out the

words. "Chase and I had made plans to meet at the barn. He wanted to check on Rafe's horse."

Chase took Laura's hand. "I couldn't be there and had asked Brent to let her know."

"I never got the message," Laura stated. "When I arrived, I waved to Lance and entered the barn through the side door. But Chase wasn't there...."

"Go on, Ms. Embry," Bradley instructed.

"Laura," she insisted. With a deep breath, she began her story again, this time determined to finish. "Brent threatened to rape me. I—"

"Rape you?" Tyler's brows drew together in a frown.

Laura couldn't look at Chase, instead she took her hand from his and focused on twisting her fingers. "I knew no one would believe me. I barely believed it myself. Brent was rich, good-looking. He could have any woman he wanted. Why would he attack me?"

"Exactly," Tyler muttered.

Bradley made notes on his pad. "Rape is about power—not sex. Go on, Laura."

Laura risked a glance at Chase then wished she hadn't after seeing the anger and compassion warring in his eyes. "Why didn't you tell me this before?"

"What was the point? I wasn't sure I was coming back. Why say bad things about your brother?"

The Senator cleared his throat, the command and hostility in his tone unmistakable. "Why *did* you come back?"

She stared at the floor, wondering if she should have run. It seemed that since that night, whatever she did was wrong. "Chase convinced me to return."

She hated Chase having to take sides and hoped her words would ease the thick tension in the room. No doubt the Senator thought his son a traitor, but she had to give him credit, under the most trying of circumstances the man was trying to be fair.

Bradley eyed the Senator who remained still as stone. "If Brent tried to rape her, she acted in self-defense. That's clear."

"So clear it took her—" Tyler jerked his thumb at her "—two years to realize it."

"Nothing is clear," Chase argued, his tone revealing his frustration. "Why would our brother attack my girl?"

"Maybe he didn't. There's only her word that Brent attacked her," Tyler said. "Maybe she attacked him."

Chase drilled Tyler with a scowl. "And her motive for attacking Brent was?"

Tyler shrugged. "Maybe Brent didn't want you two to marry. Maybe he tried to talk her into breaking things off. Maybe—"

"Maybe my foot," Laura interrupted. "You weren't there and are merely speculating."

"Well, the autopsy report revealed he was drunk and that supports her story," Bradley countered.

An odd look came into the Senator's eyes as if he were looking into the past, as if he knew something that the rest of them didn't. But he remained silent and Laura suspected he wouldn't reach a conclusion until she finished her story.

"Brent had this wild look in his eyes. He threatened to brand Rafe's foal and he frightened me. I grabbed the pitchfork to defend myself. I was hoping he'd back off.''

''You thought our brother would back off from a challenge?'' Tyler scoffed. ''You didn't know him very well.''

''Maybe I knew him better than you did. He stumbled forward and the pitchfork went in.'' She finally dared to meet the Senator's eyes that were dark, dangerous, devastatingly enraged. ''I couldn't let him hurt me.''

Tyler nudged Chase with his elbow. ''You believe her story?''

Chase locked gazes with his father and tension crackled between them. It took a full minute before he answered Tyler's question. ''Yes. I believe her.'' Laura took comfort from his words. At least Chase had given her that. He didn't think she'd lied. ''Brent had difficulty dealing with pressure. Twice, I caught him working the horses, his breath near strong enough to crack a mirror.''

Tyler shook his head. ''Lots of folks get drunk on Saturday night—''

''This was Friday afternoon.''

''—but drinking too much is a far cry from being a rapist. Suttons don't attack women, especially not their brother's woman.''

''Well, this Sutton did,'' Laura said.

''Young lady,'' the Senator drew all attention to himself, ''are you willing to take a lie detector test?''

''Yes.''

''No,'' Bradley advised. ''First, the evidence is not admissible in court. And second, the machines are only as accurate as the person administering the test is skilled.''

The Senator looked from Chase to Laura, his gaze settling on her. ''You never said *how* or *why* Chase convinced you to return.''

Uncomfortable with the way the conversation had turned, Laura hesitated. She would have preferred to tell the Senator about his grandson under less hostile conditions. But since she had an appointment with the sheriff next, she might never have a better chance to tell him than right now. ''Chase said...he didn't want...'' The words stuck in her throat. The room remained tense, silent as everyone waited for her to regain her composure. ''That night I took one of those home pregnancy tests and I was so happy it was positive.''

''Positive?'' Tyler glanced at her flat stomach as if he expected to see a baby there over two years later.

''I couldn't wait to tell Chase. Then he wasn't there and Brent attacked me. I couldn't let him hurt our baby.''

Bradley scribbled furiously, obviously pleased with her revelation. She supposed her statement would make it easier for him to defend her. He turned to a new page and paused his pen over the paper. ''So you were pregnant that night? You have medical proof?''

''I...we have a son.''

''I have a grandson?'' The Senator's voice rose in surprise, his eyebrow rising in an expression identical to one of Chase's.

Father and son exchanged hopeful looks. Chase

nodded, giving credence to her words. "Your grandson is fifteen months old."

A bright gleam shined in the Senator's eyes, but he didn't say a word. His gaze shifted to Laura's face and she swallowed hard as she read happiness and sorrow in his eyes.

"That changes nothing," Tyler argued.

"Of course it does. She's the mother of my son," Chase argued heatedly, directing his anger at Tyler—not his father who still looked shocked by her announcement.

What had she done? Laura knew the Senator well enough to understand that he considered children and grandchildren a legacy for the future. He'd often told his sons how he expected them each to marry and carry on the proud family traditions that he'd drilled into them since childhood.

"Do you have a picture?" the Senator asked her, and she could only imagine the effort it had taken for him to make his request sound casual.

Beside her, Chase stiffened and as she dug into her purse in search of a snapshot, she realized again that she'd deprived these men of family—for her son was just as much a part of them as he was a part of her. Laura pulled two pictures from her wallet and handed one each to father and grandfather. If they noticed her trembling fingers, neither of them commented on it.

Tyler didn't glance at the snapshots. A tear formed in the corner of Chase's eye and he didn't bother to wipe it away. Laura's throat tightened around a lump as she dared a glance at the Senator who stared hard at the baby picture. "You sure he's—"

"Mine?" Clearly insulted by the innuendo that the child might not be his, Chase shoved to his feet, fists clenching and unclenching with tension.

Laura jumped between them. "Stop it. The child is Chase's, but if you doubt my word, I'll agree to a DNA test."

"That won't be necessary," Chase told her.

The Senator couldn't take his eyes off the photograph. "Establishing paternity might be necessary if we have to fight her parents for custody."

Chase put his arm over Laura's shoulders. "This is our decision."

Without asking for permission to keep the picture, the Senator put the photo in his front shirt pocket. "When the press gets scent of this scandal, they're going to be sniffing for blood."

Chapter Four

The Senator and Tyler walked out of Bradley's office, turning their backs and shutting the door behind them with a quiet click of finality. Laura had expected no more—but their reaction still hurt as much as a slap. The Senator had known her since she'd been a child when she'd been a frequent guest in his home, and he'd just turned his back on her as if she were a stranger.

Laura glanced at her attorney who had a satisfied smile of triumph on his lips, as if he'd just fought a battle and won. She'd known of Bradley's reputation for being smart, but she hadn't known he could be tough, too. Not many men in this state were willing to take on the Senator.

She should be thrilled that Bradley thought her child could help her at the trial. She should feel hope that the trial might not be a travesty of justice, because thanks to Bradley's new confidence, she saw the slight possibility of a future free of prison bars.

Yet how could she feel relief when Chase's family had turned against him? He should have left with them and found a woman worthy of the Sutton name. A woman with whom he could build a dynasty to match his father's.

But Chase remained seated and as the door shut, cutting him off from his family, he stared straight ahead, focused inwardly, his back ramrod stiff. The corded muscles of his neck bunched, his shoulders straining against his black cotton shirt and his face looking loaded to the muzzle with rage. But it was his stillness that worried her the most. She wasn't sure if he was angry with her, his family or himself, and it didn't really matter, not when he'd insisted on siding with her.

He could have walked out that door with his father and brother. Instead, he'd chosen to stay. With her. She could only imagine what the gesture had cost him. Suttons always stuck together.

Even as far back as third grade, the Sutton boys were a force to be reckoned with. Todd Parker, the third-grade class bully had learned that lesson the hard way. Believing himself invincible, Parker terrorized the other kids at will and for no apparent reason, one day Parker planted his fist in Chase's face. Chase fought back but was no match for the much bigger boy. While the other kids didn't like Parker, no one dared help Chase, fearful they'd suffer the same punishment. But Parker hadn't counted on Sutton solidarity and the same afternoon of Chase's beating, Brent, Tyler, Chase, Rafe and even Cameron paid Parker a visit. While Parker was bigger than the oldest Sutton boy, he didn't stand a chance against all of them.

The Suttons had maintained that same unity all through school. No one picked on a Sutton unless one was ready to take on all five brothers. And as they grew into tall, strapping men, fights broke out less and less often. Taking on one Sutton could be daunting, but taking on all five was sheer stupidity.

That solidarity extended to other facets of ranch life. They'd all learned at an early age that their roots grew thick and strong in the land that supported their cattle. The land was home and the land would always endure—just like the Sutton family. The Sutton brothers attended church together. Partied together. No one in Highview would think of throwing a barbecue and inviting one Sutton and not the others. The family was a team.

And because of Laura, the Suttons now considered Chase a traitor. Because of her, the Senator had never held his grandson. And because of her, Chase had been forced to stand against the family he loved. As much as she ached for him to stay with her, she didn't want to cause him more heartache.

Placing her hand on top of his, she squeezed lightly. "Maybe you should go."

Chase studied her for a moment, intently. She made herself hold his gaze and watched his determination harden. Then slowly, his eyes focused on Bradley. "Are we done here?"

Bradley checked his watch. "For now. The sheriff's expecting us."

The walk across the street to the sheriff's office was all too short. Thankfully, the nondescript building was empty except for a deputy who ushered them past the dispatcher into a windowless room that lacked furniture except a scarred table and hard chairs. Within moments, the sheriff joined them.

Laura had known Sheriff Noel Demory since childhood. A short man with a rangy thin body, he made up for in smarts what he lacked in stature. He kept a low profile around town, preventing trouble before it started while maintaining an amiable eye on the locals. Given his popularity with Highview's citizens, no one had bothered to run against him at election time.

He didn't stand for drugs or gambling and he sure didn't countenance murder. She suspected that Noel might have taken her running away as a personal slight, but she wouldn't have known it by his expression.

He held out his hand to Bradley. "Howdy."

"Sheriff," said Chase, taking his turn at shaking hands with Noel. The two men knew one another well, and it was a measure of the sheriff's respect for the Suttons that he didn't question Chase's right to remain.

Noel's sharp gaze moved from Bradley to Chase to Laura. "You did the right thing coming back."

"I hope so." While Laura suspected the sheriff was forcing friendliness to take her off her guard, she had to make herself hold still in order not to fidget under his scrutiny.

Noel gestured for them to take seats. "Anyone want coffee or a soda?"

Laura's mouth had gone dry at the thought of having to tell her story once more. "I'd like a glass of water, please."

Noel brought her lukewarm water in a paper cup. She sipped, grateful for the tiny delay. Then slowly, she repeated her story, Bradley coaching her on some of the details.

Noel listened without interrupting, making notes on a legal pad. When she finished, he clicked the top of his pen and frowned. "Isn't it unusual to brand a horse in a barn? Couldn't that cause a fire?"

"Brent was drunk." Laura nodded, trying to gauge whether or not Noel believed her or was merely trying to trip her up but she couldn't read his expression. "I threw a bucket of water on the branding iron."

"Tell me about the pitchfork."

She crumpled the empty paper cup in her hand. "What about it?" Her voice must have sounded as tight as she felt because Chase reached over, removed the paper cup from her clenched fingers and took her hand. She hung on tight, drinking in his warmth, his strength.

Noel looked from his notes to her. "How were you holding the pitchfork?"

"By the handle."

"Was it upright or sideways?"

What difference did it make? But something was biting at Noel. Squeezing Chase's hand hard, she answered as exactly as she could. "I held the pitchfork upright. The tines pointed toward Brent. I was resting the handle on the floor."

"You're sure?"

"Pretty sure."

"Noel," Bradley interrupted with a tinge of impatience, "where're you going with this?"

"Just satisfying my curiosity." Noel scratched his bald head. "And how many times did you stab Brent?"

"I didn't stab him. He tripped and fell toward me."

"And you lifted the pitchfork off the ground?"

"I don't think so." She'd been too scared to move. She'd frozen.

"Where did the tines enter the body?"

"His chest."

"You sure?"

How could she forget? She recalled the blood seeping through his shirt. The fear slaking through her that she hadn't injured him badly enough and he might yet rise again to threaten her. But he hadn't moved because she'd killed him. "Yes, I'm sure. Why?"

"Okay, so let me get this straight. He fell into the pitchfork and it stabbed his chest. You didn't stab him twice?"

Frustration made the words hard to say. "He dropped to...the ground. He was...dead. Why... would I...stab him again?"

The sheriff handed her a file. "According to the autopsy report, Brent Sutton died from a pitchfork wound to the throat."

The throat?

Numb, Laura opened the file and glanced at a picture taken of Brent at the time of death. His eyes stared open in accusation, his head tilted back as he lay in the straw barn. At his bare neck, she plainly saw dark tine marks and blood.

Astounded, Laura snapped the folder closed and squirmed in her chair. Her thoughts whirled in crazy circles with the multiple ramifications. Even after taking a deep, steadying breath, she could barely take in what she'd just seen and what the sheriff had just told her.

Brent had died from a throat wound. But she'd stabbed his chest. It didn't make sense.

Bradley jumped to his feet and paced. "Noel, I haven't had time to study the autopsy report. Did Brent die from the throat wounds?"

"The chest wounds were superficial. The deep ones in his throat killed him."

She wasn't a killer. Laura's eyes filled with tears she couldn't blink back. For two long years she'd had to live with the guilt of ending a life, a burden that had cost her dearly. She'd told herself she'd acted in self-defense and that Brent hadn't given her a choice. But all the logic in the world hadn't stopped her from endlessly speculating over what she'd done wrong that night, what she could have done differently. Maybe she should have screamed or tried to run. But she always came back to the same conclusion—she'd had no choice.

Cold logic had never put out the burning knot of guilt in her heart, but the sheriff's matter-of-fact statements had doused the flaming guilt in her soul. She wasn't a killer. Not in self-defense. Not even accidentally.

Tears of happiness and relief running down her cheek, she turned to Chase and realized he was looking at her in a way that matched the relief she was feeling inside, as if he were as eager to hear the words as she was to say them. "I didn't kill him. I'm not a murderer."

Bradley threaded his fingers through his gray hair. "Now all we have to do is prove it."

A knock was followed by the blond-haired dispatcher's entrance into the room. Her eyes glanced from the autopsy report on the table then to Laura's and Chase's joined hands before reporting with professional authority to her boss, "Sorry, Noel but I just dispatched your last two black and whites, one to a domestic disturbance, the second to a swimming pool accident. And a minute ago I took a frantic phone call from a citizen who claims a drunk driver is weaving through downtown.''

"Francesca, I'll be with you in a minute.'' The sheriff dismissed the dispatcher, waited until she'd closed the door behind her and turned to Bradley. ''You've got your work cut out for you. You have only Laura's word against incriminating evidence. There was only one set of prints on the pitchfork. Laura's. And the ranch hand witnessed only one person fleeing the crime scene. Laura.''

"ALL RISE FOR the Honorable Judge Perkins.''

At the bailiff's words, the buzzing low murmurs of Highviews's citizens ceased. Within the crowded courtroom, papers rustled, throats cleared and a child cried out before his mother hushed him with a gentle caress. The murder case was the first in these parts in years and anything that involved Senator Sutton was news. Highview's premier reporter, Mac Nolan, took notes while an artist sketched. Even Judge Stewart had entered the courtroom to listen to his old partner argue for bail.

Chase divided his attention between Laura and the Senator who'd slipped into the courtroom as the crowd rose to their feet. Tyler must have headed back to the ranch but the Senator wasn't alone. Cameron had flown in from Boston, to be with the family during this crisis, and Chase was thankful. Where Tyler had a good heart, his temper tended to get the best of him; Cameron was a rock who refrained from voicing his opinions until he'd thought out

every fork in the road. Brilliant, decisive and com-
passionate in a crisis, Cam was the brother Chase
would pick to back him right up to hell's front door.

The two brothers exchanged nods of greeting over
the heads of the restless crowd and then Chase
turned forward comforted by Cam's composed presence. Knowing the Senator wasn't alone allowed
Chase to focus on Laura who stood slightly to the
side and in front of him, next to Bradley.

With her face pale and her expression rigid, Laura
fidgeted with her purse strap, her restless fingers betraying frazzled nerves. Chase had dreaded this moment ever since she'd agreed to return to Highview.
He couldn't imagine what she must be feeling,
knowing that she might have to wait behind bars for
her trial, especially now that she knew she hadn't
killed Brent. At least the Senator had pulled strings
to have their case moved to the top of the docket.

Lots of old connections in this room. The sheriff
had taken over the job two decades ago and knew
all the players. Both of the sheriff's deputies were
in court along with the dispatcher, and Chase wondered briefly who was minding the store. Judge
Stewart, dressed in a designer suit and tie, his thin-
ning hair slicked in a comb-over to hide his balding
head, stood in the back and again Chase was surprised by his interest. Although he was Bradley's
old law partner, his main interests these days were
in Denver.

Bradley's dark-haired secretary Sally Walker was
scribbling notes. At least Bradley appeared to be
taking the crowd in stride, but then he'd been trying
cases before Perkins for years, so no doubt he knew
the district attorney quite well.

The bailiff handed Judge Perkins a file. The judge must be close to eighty, Chase figured, but there was no sign his cinch was frayed. The man's bright blue eyes were as clear and deep as a reflecting pool. "Please be seated."

Chase gave Laura a look of encouragement. As the rest of the room sat, Laura, Bradley and the district attorney walked forward. Laura's back was straight, her chin high, but Chase sensed the effort just standing there cost her.

Judge Perkins wasted no time, peering at Laura through gold-rimmed bifocals. "Laura Embry, you have been charged with second degree murder. How do you plead?"

Laura spoke quietly but firmly. "Not guilty, Your Honor."

Perkins nodded and looked to the district attorney. "Counselor?"

The D.A. straightened his tie and strode forward pompously. "Ms. Embry's fingerprints were on the murder weapon. She was seen leaving the crime scene. Law enforcement has been searching for her for two years, Your Honor. We ask that the court deny bail."

Several people in the crowd around Chase vented anger with shocked gasps, a few curse words and one couple broke into a noisy argument. Laura might have been gone for two years but she obviously still had friends in Highview.

The judge smacked his gavel. "We'll have order or I'll have the courtroom cleared."

At the threat, people turned quiet. Chase noted the shudder that went through Laura, but she remained stiff, shoulders squared. At her distress, he restrained a string of cuss words that would sizzle bacon. He hated seeing her go through this proceeding, and he couldn't imagine what a full-blown trial would do to her.

Although she clearly had friends ready to defend her, she wouldn't want them seeing her humiliation—especially if this hearing didn't go her way and the bailiff took her to jail in handcuffs. Chase almost wished Perkins would clear the courtroom, but the crowd stayed quiet.

Satisfied, the judge nodded at Laura's attorney. "Mr. Bradley?"

"Ms. Embry has roots in this community. Her family lives here. Her grandfather—"

"Kane Embry, God rest his soul," Perkins bristled with irritation, his impatient stare drilling Bradley, "would turn over in his grave if he knew his granddaughter stood before me accused of murder. Him and me—we go way back. So don't waste my time on a history lesson."

While Judge Perkins had supported the Senator, he also had ties to the Embrys. Chase wondered if this would be a difficult case for him to try, yet never doubted he would do his best to remain impartial. Perkins might be touchy but he was fair.

"Yes, sir." Without pausing, Bradley continued, "Ms. Embry has never been in trouble with the law and she's no danger to the community."

"I object," the D.A. almost shouted. "She stabbed Brent Sutton with a pitchfork and—"

"In this country," Bradley spoke mildly, his soft words effective, "one is still innocent until proven guilty."

The D.A. threw his arms wide, pointing in the

general direction of the jail. "She belongs behind bars. She fled the crime scene, changed her identity—"

"And returned of her own volition," Bradley argued.

Perkins banged his gavel. "Enough! I'm setting bail at five hundred thousand dollars." He turned to the bailiff. "Next case."

The courtroom exploded into a cacophony of shouts, swear words and movement. Chase took one look at the strain on Laura's face, stepped forward and smoothly grabbed her elbow in case she fainted.

"It's okay," he murmured, keeping his voice pitched as if he were calming a spooked foal.

"No, it's not." Her voice broke. "We don't have that kind of money."

"Your father can put up the ranch as collateral."

Laura should her head, and the pain he saw in her face made his knees go weak. "You don't understand. After last year's drought, he needed cash to buy more stock. Dad intends to repay the loan after summer roundup."

"And he had to buy a new hay baler," Chase recalled with a plummeting sensation in his gut, knowing ranch equipment came dear and that ranching made for a good life but a poor living.

"Right now, the bank owns more of the ranch than we do." She lifted her head, her eyes stark with agony, but she looked him in the eye as the bailiff came to take her away. "Goodbye, Chase. Take care of our son."

"WHEN I THANKED Judge Stewart for putting up my bail money, he said it was because he and my grandfather were friends," Laura told Chase, trying to distract herself from the empty ache inside her as she watched Chase hold her son. For fifteen months she'd taken care of Keith alone. She knew her son's habits, his smile and that loud noises frightened him. Giving him into Chase's care hadn't been easy, yet she knew it was better for father and son to get to know one another while she was around to help. Although reluctant to bring up any subject that could spoil their first horseback ride as a family, Laura couldn't get over Judge Stewart having paid her bail.

But then many people had whispered warm words of encouragement in her ear. Bradley's secretary had told her to hang in there. One of the deputies had mentioned that she'd picked a terrific attorney. Even the dispatcher, Francesca Martin had insisted Bradley could win her case and it pleased Laura that not everyone in town thought she was guilty. Forcing her stiff shoulders to relax, she tried to enjoy the ride.

Tall in the saddle, Chase wrapped his arm around Keith's waist, cradling the toddler between his strong thighs. A bright red bandanna around his neck accented his broad shoulders above a collarless shirt of navy cotton. Both Laura and Chase wore chaps to protect their legs and horses' flanks. And Chase had added a vest, his black pockets bulging with baby cookies and Keith's pacifier.

With a chuckle of delight, Keith let go of the pommel and patted the horse's withers. "Horsey."

"Judge Stewart is no friend of the Senator's."

Chase's response jerked her back from her momentary pride at Keith's growing vocabulary. Laura shifted in the saddle, knowing muscles she hadn't used in over two years would be sore tomorrow. She tilted back her Stetson, and with a mother's protectiveness watched Chase balance Keith. "You're saying I've accepted help from the enemy?"

Aware of her scrutiny, Chase merely shrugged. He reached forward and disentangled Keith's hand from the horse's mane, easily keeping track of his son, his horse and the conversation—an unusual trait for a man. "Could be Judge Stewart wanted to rile the Senator."

"Why?"

"Maybe he plans to run against him during the next election. Or maybe he didn't like the way Dad voted on a bill." Chase's eyes scanned the gentle trail ahead, tightening his grip on Keith.

Laura held her breath as a jackrabbit bolted across their path. Chase's steady mount didn't so much as flinch.

Deciding Keith couldn't be in better hands, Laura tugged her hat brim over her forehead to shade her eyes from the setting sun. "I asked my parents if Judge Stewart and my granddaddy were close, but neither of them could recall. Bradley said just to let it go and instead start thinking about who had access to the Sutton barn."

Chase snorted. "We don't lock it."

"If I didn't kill Brent, then someone else did. The only other person I saw that night was Lance."

"He's loyal."

"You think Lance could have entered the barn after I left and an injured Brent attacked him—believing it was me?"

"And Lance stabbed Brent in the throat with a

pitchfork?'' Chase's skepticism carried clearly over the clop of the horses' hooves.

Despite Chase having shot down her theory, Laura couldn't get too upset. For the first time today, she let herself live in the moment, breathed in deeply, relished the clean air. Until this ride she hadn't realized how much she'd missed Colorado. The sweet grass between towering mountains, the gentle wind, the gray sky as velvety as her sorrel's muzzle. This was Embry land. Her grandfather's father had homesteaded the place. Granddaddy had turned it into a working cattle ranch and her father had hung on to the land through the drought and recession. Embrys would always live here—even if she couldn't raise her son, Keith would know his roots.

Her child pointed to a lazily circling eagle. ''Bird. Big, big bird.''

''Eagle,'' Chase told him.

''E-ll,'' Keith repeated.

Chase would see that their child grew up strong and proud and that he'd learn there was nothing more important than family.

Family.

The Suttons were closer than a wolf pack breathing down her neck. She couldn't bear to ask Chase if, after sticking by her side through the courtroom ordeal today, he'd alienated himself from his brothers and his father, perhaps forever.

He'd seemed preoccupied since the ride began, almost focused within himself as if his mind were elsewhere. Even his conversation seemed perfunctory if not forced. In fact he acted naturally only with Keith.

"Hold up," Chase ordered. With two hands he lifted the toddler from the saddle and turned him until Keith's drooping head rested on Chase's shoulder. "This little guy is tuckered out. We should head back."

"You go. I told Dad I'd check the fence line at Sutton Ferry."

Although sandbars had made the river more shallow and no ferry carried livestock across the river that bordered the two ranches anymore, the name of the spit of land jutting into the river had stuck from the popular ferry crossing of a hundred years past. Embry cattle often broke through the barbed wire fence, eager to drink in the river. Afterward, the cows had a way of wandering onto Sutton land.

In past years when there had been no tensions between the ranches, the Suttons had shooed the Embry cattle back. But Dad said lately they had losses he couldn't account for and that worried Laura. Rustling was ugly business and tensions between the neighbors were riding high. None of them needed more trouble.

As well as Chase was doing with the baby, Laura had no fear of leaving Keith alone with him, but was saddened that she could be replaced so easily. She squelched her jealousy, telling herself she should be glad that Keith had accepted the move out west, his grandparents and his father.

Chase looked uncomfortable at her suggestion to separate, his eyes narrowing. "We could come back together."

Her head jerked up and she noted the fires banked in his eyes. So he wasn't indifferent to her after all. Was he remembering the last time they'd made love

and the site of Keith's conception that was just up
this trail another mile or two?

"I'm used to being alone now." She let him
down gently. The last thing she needed was another
complication. Besides, even if she had been inclined
to fan the embers in his eyes, she wasn't a free
woman. She could very well have to spend the rest
of her life behind bars. The sheriff's words haunted
her. Just because she now knew she was innocent
of murder didn't mean she could prove it.

"You've been a city girl for two years. You sure
you'll be okay out here by yourself?"

Laura patted the rifle strapped to her saddle. "I
haven't forgotten how to use this." Before Chase
could utter another reason why she should return
with him, before he could read her eyes and realize
that she ached to bathe Keith, smooth his silky skin
and put him to bed herself, she lightly dug her heels
into her mount.

The obliging horse took off into a canter, but she
slowed him after the first bend. Dusk came early in
the mountains and although she remembered this
trail as well as her mother's kitchen, she had to
watch out for rock slides, darting deer, possums and
skunks or the rare coyote.

Cows, horses, grass, rain and land. These elements once defined her existence. She'd missed
moving cattle from one pasture to another, missed
doctoring a sick calf or birthing a foal. Before her
part-time education had been interrupted at the community college, she'd studied animal science and
agricultural economics and learned how to use a
computer to keep the books.

She'd always intended to urge her father into diversification to keep the ranch profitable. She and Chase had spent hours considering the merits of leasing acreage to hunters versus selling breeding stock. Chase had sometimes volunteered to do double duty as tour guide when cash was short.

And since tourism accounted for the most profitable ventures in Highview, they'd racked their brains for ways to tap into the lucrative market. Laura had put her foot down over offering dude ranching facilities, wanting to keep the land private. Chase had even suggested stocking giraffes, zebras and other exotic game to offer safari-style photographic hunts to visitors.

Laura grinned at the thought as she urged her mount around the last bend before arriving at Sutton's Ferry. As she rode over the path she knew so well, a sense of well-being infused her with new determination. She ached to spend the rest of her life here and watch her son grow into a man. But to do that, she had to find Brent's killer. Before today, everyone had believed her guilty—herself included. But now that she knew she hadn't killed Chase's brother, she had to find a way to clear her name.

Under a crescent moon, the river rippled before her. Sure enough, the cows had broken through the barbed wire, pulled down a fence post and stood drinking along the riverbank.

Laura went to work, moving as one with her horse to drive the cows back where they belonged. An hour later, she dismounted and shoved the fence post back into the hole, gave it a couple of whacks with a crowbar she kept in her saddlebags and kicked in some dirt. Last, she tromped on the dirt with her boot heel. Stringing barbed wire was as ornery a job a rancher could find. The barbs tended to get stuck on one another. After slipping on a pair of bull-hide gloves, she twisted the broken stands back together with a pair of pliers, knowing the fix was temporary.

She'd remounted, ready to head for home when three gunshots blasted into the air. Her horse whinnied but didn't panic, the shots having been fired from miles away.

Out west three shots signaled trouble and were a call for help. Laura rode as hard as she dared for the nearest rise and pulled out her cell phone. Although Chase and Keith should have been home a long time ago, she wanted to check on their safety. "Mom? I heard three shots. Is everything okay?"

"Yes, dear. Keith's sleeping and Chase rode over to the Sutton ranch. He said something about checking employment records two years back. And Mark Bradley called earlier and I told him you were out for a ride."

Relief that her son and folks seemed fine couldn't override the prickles of tension coursing through her. "Okay, I'll ride up to Embry Peak and look around."

"Be careful, dear."

Laura ended the call quickly, intent on saving her batteries. She made a mental note to transfer her service to Colorado so every time she phoned it didn't route through Louisiana and back.

The short ride up the bare peak gave her a 360 degree view for miles around. She let her horse cool down and took out her binoculars. First, she focused on the Embry ranch. It looked normal.

Sometimes cars broke down miles from town so

she perused the road into town for as far as she could see. Nothing.

All of a sudden, every light at the Sutton Barn flared, inside illumination as well as outside floodlights. And Laura had a drowning feeling in the pit of her stomach. Mom had said Chase had ridden over there.

She'd hoped he'd joined in on the Senator's county-famous poker game that usually included the sheriff, several judges and visiting dignitaries. She prayed Chase wasn't in that Sutton barn, or had put himself in danger by asking someone the wrong questions.

Chapter Five

Thirty minutes late, Laura skidded to a halt outside the Sutton barn, tossed the reins over her horse's head and leapt to the ground. Her weak knees barely held as she staggered past the red-and-blue swirling lights of the sheriff's car, an ambulance and assorted pickup trucks.

"Chase!"

Please be okay.

Blinking at the bright lights inside the barn, she didn't waste a moment to allow her eyes to adjust but raced forward. Many ranchers settled for a prefabricated wooden loose box with a tack room and feed shed for a barn. But the Sutton's stable, with central heating and air-conditioning, boasted rows of first-class boxes divided by a center passageway with sliding main doors for exit and entrance at each end. Right now, the spacious center aisle was crowded with onlookers that stood aside to give paramedics room to work on someone.

She shoved through the Sutton hands, past women who mucked out stalls, their grim faces warning her that the sight ahead would not be pleasant. Swallow-

ing the clogged fear in her throat, she made herself
look at the fallen man.

Chase? Dark hair over his forehead, an oxygen
mask over his face, eyes closed and skin a sickly
gray, he looked more dead than alive.

"Chase!" A deputy kept her from going to him.
"Is he okay? What happened? Will he be all right?"

Strong, familiar arms wrapped around her.
Chase's arms. He was okay. That wasn't him lying
so still and gray on the floor but another Sutton.

She flung herself against his chest. "I thought it
was you and—"

"It's Tyler."

"Oh, God. I heard the shots that signalled for help
all the way out at Sutton Ferry."

"Lance fired three shots when he found Tyler,"
Chase explained.

"I saw the barn lights and I had to come. I
thought something had…" She closed her mouth,
stopping her panicked babbling. She'd been so worried over Chase, was so glad to feel him, touch him,
breathe in his musky scent, she hadn't yet thought
to worry over his brother.

Another Sutton brother.

Without pulling back from Chase, her gaze found
the Senator sitting on a bench, his elbows on his
knees, his head bowed, face in his hands. She prayed
he hadn't just lost another son. But Tyler had been
breathing or they wouldn't have kept the oxygen
mask on his face. Even now she could hear the hiss
of air going in and out. Had one of the horses kicked
Tyler? Why didn't Chase tell her what had happened?

The sheriff separated himself from the group of

men staring at her that included Lance, the ranch hand who'd been here the night Brent died, Judges Stewart and Perkins, Mark Bradley, Mac Nolan the reporter, Cameron and Rafe Sutton who looked even taller and thinner than the last time she'd seen him.

The sheriff took her elbow. "We need to talk. Do you want your attorney?"

Chopper blades interrupted the conversation. Paramedics lifted Tyler's stretcher and carried him to the waiting chopper where he would be airlifted to Denver. All the serious injuries flew into the big city. Cameron climbed into the chopper, too, and the helicopter took off. Damn! Tyler must be hurt bad.

The sheriff gestured Bradley to join her and Chase, leading them away from the others. She shot a quick look at Chase and saw nothing but pain in his eyes. No suspicion. No sign of mistrust. No anger.

And she was more confused than ever. "Why do I need Bradley? Would somebody tell me what the hell is going on?"

"I'd advise you not to say a word," Bradley whispered in her ear.

The sheriff watched her face. "Tyler stepped in a mud puddle. An electrified puddle."

Laura frowned. "I don't understand."

"Ms. Embry," Bradley insisted, his round face looking at her kindly. "I can't help you if you insist on talking to the sheriff."

She drew away from her attorney sure she could straighten out this misunderstanding. "I have nothing to hide."

Chase pointed to a wire coming from the tack room. "Someone broke into the barn, hot-wired a

220 volt line from the water pump, dropped one end in the puddle and covered the wire with hay to hide it. Tyler stepped into the puddle and was…''

Zapped.

''It wasn't an accident?'' Laura looked at the sheriff and fear turned her intestines into one giant knot. ''Surely you don't think *I* had anything to do with it?''

They suspected her of trying to murder Tyler. That's why Bradley had urged her to keep quiet. Damning herself for speaking up, she had the awful suspicion things were about to get worse. Much worse.

The sheriff held up a clear plastic bag. Inside was a long strand of blond hair, hair that looked as if it matched her own. ''I found this on the water pump. My deputy is dusting for fingerprints now.''

Stunned, Laura's mind went numb but she still couldn't fathom what was happening here. ''But…but…it can't be my hair. Don't other women work in this barn?''

''None of them have the same color hair as this— nor were they around when Brent was killed,'' the sheriff said pointedly.

''How would I even know Tyler was going to step in the puddle?''

''The trap was in front of the stall of the horse he'd been working for the past two weeks. It wouldn't have been hard to learn he came out here every night after sunset.''

Adrenaline kicked in, pushing away the fuzziness. ''Why would I even want to kill Tyler?''

The sheriff's voice carried through the barn. ''Since the Senator always places the eldest son in charge, with Tyler out of the way, Chase would inherit the Sutton ranch. He's the next brother in line to take over. Maybe the two of you planned this together.''

Chase's hand tightened around hers. Laura gasped. She had to get hold of herself before she rammed a fist at the sheriff's face. It was bad enough that he thought she could have hurt Tyler, but to accuse Chase was unconscionable.

The Senator strode over, his face hard as flint. ''No Sutton would kill his own blood.''

''You got a rich spread here, Senator,'' the sheriff argued. ''There's no telling what some folks would do for—''

''Not my son.'' The fierce, predatory roar of rage in the Senator's voice, his absolute conviction in Chase's innocence brought Laura a measure of relief. Feelings between the Suttons might be running high, but they would stand together.

The sheriff knew when to back off. He tilted his thin chin toward Laura, his mouth twisted wryly. ''Maybe she did it alone. You have an alibi, ma'am?''

''I was—''

''Don't say another word,'' Bradley ordered.

Laura ignored him. If she could clear herself, she didn't want the sheriff wasting time pursuing her while the real killer was getting away. ''Chase and I were riding to Sutton Ferry. Cows broke through the fence and I rounded them up and repaired the barbed wire.''

Chase eyes lingered on her face as if trying to read her soul while the sheriff asked him, ''So you were with her? I thought you were playing poker with the your dad and his friends?''

Laura frowned, recalling that Chase had told her mother he was reviewing employment records, but she kept her confusion to herself.

Chase looked at his watch, his face bleak, his eyes haunted. ''Laura and I were together until I turned back to the Embry place and put our son to bed. Laura went on alone.''

''How much time has passed since you last saw her?'' the sheriff asked.

''Maybe an hour.''

The sheriff pursed his lips, eyeing her warily. ''More than enough time to ride over here and lay a trap for Tyler.''

''But I didn't and I have proof,'' Laura replied, hope that she could clear her name giving her voice strength.

''You do?'' the Senator sounded hopeful.

''Yes, sir. I sure do.''

''Really,'' the sheriff stepped forward as if his fervor were a physical thing pushing him. ''I haven't had a murder in Highview in two years. Since the last time *you* were in town.''

Laura swallowed hard but she didn't back down. ''There's tracks all over from my horse and herding those cows. Someone around here should be able to read the tracks and tell how old they are. And even if you can't know right to the minute, I couldn't have made that many tracks in less than the good half hour it took to round those cows up. Since the time Chase left me, I wouldn't have had time to have tracked up the riverbank, fixed the fence and then ridden over here, would I?''

"Not unless you had wings," Chase agreed.

The sheriff tipped his hat, his eyes bright with suspicion. "I'll head out to Sutton Ferry with Lance and Rafe. Those boys could follow a wood tick on solid rock. Meantime, young lady, why don't you have your attorney take you home?"

"I WANT TO talk to you," the Senator told Chase. Although he couched his words as an invitation, the tone was one of command.

Accompanying his father outside the barn where they could speak in privacy, Chase watched Bradley guide Laura into his car to take her home, but only after one on the ranch hands assured her they would take care of her horse.

She looked so frail, battered by the events of the evening. But her posture declared her innocence, the proud tilt of her head softened by eyes darkened with sadness and exhaustion, her steps weary. How many more accusations could one slight pair of shoulders bear before breaking under the strain?

"She was set up."

"I believe you." The Senator took out a cigar, snipped off the end and savored the scent as he watched the hand lasso the horses that had gotten loose through an open gate in the corral.

Chase eyed his father unable to understand him. After seeing Tyler looking like he'd saddled a cloud and ridden to the great beyond, the Senator had almost fallen apart. Another man would be rushing to his son's hospital room to see how Tyler was doing. But the Senator was a man who didn't let his emotions rule him. No doubt he'd figured that the best way to help Tyler was to look after his interests, and let the doctors inform him the moment they had news. Even now he'd straightened his backbone and stood here casually. But Chase knew him well enough to know the effort cost him. He could see the slight tremor in the Senator's fingers, hear the edge in his voice.

Chase strove to keep his own composure. "What changed your mind about Laura?"

"Instinct."

"That's it?"

The Senator clamped down on the cigar. "You know her better than any of us. If you believe she's innocent, most likely she is."

"I thank you for that."

"But there's more," his father continued, grimacing at the chaos outside as men lassoed and saddled up horses. "I don't think it was an accident those animals escaped the corral."

Shortly after Lance had discovered Tyler on the barn's floor and summoned help, he'd moved the nervous horses from the barn into a holding corral. Chase frowned. "I can't recall the last time one of our hands forgot to lock the gate. But the men might have been so worried over Tyler—"

"Or set on *delaying* the sheriff and Rafe's tracking expedition."

His father's words kicked his gut. Delay Rafe and the sheriff? Why? There could be only one reason. Someone intended to tamper with Laura's alibi.

"I wouldn't be surprised if Laura's tracks were obliterated the moment she headed our way."

Bile rose into the back of Chase's throat. He checked his watch again, realizing a good half hour had passed while they'd rounded up the loose horses.

Rafe and the sheriff had just set out at a gallop but Chase suspected their efforts would prove to be too late. Someone had tried to land Tyler in a shallow grave and wanted the blame to fall on Laura. With a bitter scowl, he suddenly realized that the hair sample from the water pump would likely match Laura's DNA. Coldly and methodically someone had set her up.

His father pulled out his cell phone and punched buttons. "We have to start thinking ahead."

"But—"

His father held up his hand, gesturing for silence and speaking into the phone. "I want the jet ready to fly to Denver at first light."

Chase shook, refusing to let himself wonder if Tyler would survive until morning. There had been room for only one Sutton on the chopper besides Tyler, and Cameron, a medical doctor, had been the best choice. Still, Chase wished he could be with Tyler now, telling him to fight, demanding he hang on.

Chase would be ready to leave in the morning. "I'm coming with you."

"Pack your funeral suit."

Unbidden, tears pricked Chase's eyes and stabbed his throat. "You don't think he'll make it? Did Cameron—"

"The best way to protect Tyler…is for everyone except our family to think he died during the helicopter ride."

What? Chase shook his head as if to clear out the dust devils. "You lost me."

"Cameron will give a fake name at the military hospital in Denver. No one there will know the patient is your brother."

"Come on, Dad. You sound crazy. Not even you can keep Tyler's accident a secret. Nurses talk, the doctors will talk."

"The public won't even suspect. Because tomorrow, we hold the funeral and cremate Tyler Sutton."

At times, his father could be as hard to pin down as smoke in a bottle. But suddenly he caught on. "We're *faking* Tyler's death?"

"It's the best way to protect him." The Senator lit his cigar, puffing smoke so strong it would derail a freight train. "Someone tried to murder my son tonight. I won't leave him lying bare-assed in a nest of rattlers. He's barely conscious."

"For how long?"

"Cameron said…maybe, a while." The Senator's voice had weakened, then hummed with fervor. "We can't let the killer try again."

A ranch hand shut off the barn's lights. The moon slipped behind a cloud and it was very dark.

Chase hesitated. "You can pull off the deception?"

"I have friends in the right places."

"And how many laws will you break?"

The Senator shrugged. "I'm harming no one, except—"

"Laura!" Chase punched his fist into his palm, his heart bleeding like a skewered hog. "We can't do this to her. She'll be arrested for committing another murder."

"It's the best option."

Not for Laura.

His father was asking him to destroy the mother

of his child with a lie. Chase went very still, his heart galloping in his chest. "Laura's case will make national headlines. Her parents and our son will never live this down."

"But she will live—which is more than I can hope for Tyler unless you help."

Chase had accused Laura of running away after Brent's murder. Of not trusting him to believe in her. And now it was he who was the one unwilling to trust Laura. Perhaps she'd been right. With the stakes upped to life and death, he found his father persuading him. As much as he hated to lie, he couldn't afford to jeopardize Tyler's life.

"Wait! Maybe...I could tell her and she could pretend—"

"No!"

"Dad, I trust her."

His father placed a hand on Chase's shoulder. "Suppose we're both wrong about her? You can't risk your brother's life."

"There must be another way."

"Find the killer. I could help, pull some strings with the FBI, but a leak that I'm helping Laura could alert the killer. He could go to ground."

"For all we know," Chase muttered in frustration, "the killer could be halfway to Hawaii by now."

"I'm betting that he stuck around and freed those horses. He intends to stay in Highview and let Laura take the blame."

"Suppose you're wrong, Dad?"

"Suppose I'm right?"

"You want me to lie to Laura. Pretend my brother is dead." The plan sickened him. The lies and the coverup would give the Embry family even more trouble than Job.

"I've already spoken to the sheriff to make this as easy on her as possible. He's agreed not to arrest Laura until after the DNA results on the hair sample come back. That should buy you some time."

"And what'll Laura think once she learns the truth? That I let the whole world believe her a two-time killer because I didn't trust her enough to—" His voice broke.

"With Tyler gone, I need your help here. Perhaps you should come home for a while."

"And abandon Laura?" Bitterness, thick and sour and clotted, welled in him. "It's not enough you want me to lie to her, you want me to just up and desert her, too?"

"I'm sorry."

His father's apology glanced off him. "Put Rafe in charge here."

His father puffed his cigar, his tone certain. "He's not ready."

Chase threw his arms wide. "No one's ready to run this place." His father had the old-fashioned notion that one man should run the ranch. But the Sutton acreage was the size of a small town with problems their ancestors never had to deal with. While horses remained the favorite mode of transportation, cowboys carried out daily chores on snowmobiles, trucks and helicopters and the vehicles needed steady maintenance. Computers had entered the offices and required educated people to run them. And the ranch land was now often subdivided or rented out as cattle prices rose and fell. Condominiums and modern subdivisions had crept into the valley and

the loud engines of recreational tourist vehicles too
often terrorized cattle and ruined good grazing land.
Trespassers on horseback or foot could cause even
more damage. Running the Sutton operation had
grown too big for one man to handle.

Chase's jaw tightened. "The job drove Brent to
drink, Tyler to exhaustion."

"I need you."

Disgusted with his father's stubbornness, Chase
turned his back and walked away. "Find someone
else."

CHASE FOUND LAURA on the comfortable swing on
the Embry front porch. She sat in the dark, soft and
quiet, hugging her knees, staring at the night sky.
Out here in the specter of the San Juan mountains
and without the city lights to dim them, the stars
looked close enough to touch, bright enough to see
by.

Shadows in her eyes, Laura lifted her head and
waited for him to sit next to her before breaking the
silence. "How's Tyler?"

The lie caught in Chase's throat. "We don't know
anything yet."

Laura took his hand and squeezed. "He's going
to be okay. I can feel it."

Moved by her attempt to cheer him, horrified by
what the lie would do to her, Chase said nothing.
Instead he gathered her against his chest until her
head rested in the crook of his shoulder and he
breathed in her scent, a fragrant mix of femininity,
saddle soap and leather.

"You heard from Rafe?" she asked, looking toward Sutton Ferry.

He shook his head, fighting the inner heat that just holding her caused him. He had no right to take any more from her—not since he planned to follow through on the Senator's lie. But she felt so comfortable in his arms, so right, it was if they were meant to be together.

His jeans tightened and he shifted, knowing she shouldn't be having this effect of him. Not with one brother in his grave and the other badly injured. But he was alive damn it, and he couldn't quite let her go.

He drew in a deep gulp of air, trying to slow his breathing. And his spinning thoughts. He didn't understand this attraction between them that was so much more than sex. Sex was a pleasant pastime between two consenting adults. Sometimes it was self-indulgent. But never, ever had it felt so necessary to life—except with Laura.

She snuggled against his side as if unaware of the inner battle that raged inside him, the soft curve of her breast brushing his chest, her silky hair teasing his nostrils with a lemon scent. He searched for and couldn't find the strength to pull away. So he took the coward's way out. Closing his eyes, he waited, tense and immobile, expecting her to take his stillness as rejection and move away.

But his silence and aloofness didn't frighten her away. She tilted her head up to him and his eyes opened. Before she could ask another question that he didn't want to answer, he lowered his head, his lips nibbling hers. She tasted sweeter than fresh cream over ripe strawberries.

Something hot and powerful leapt inside him, kindled fierce hard sparks that set him ablaze with need.

Passion he'd kept rigidly controlled, strictly ignored, strained free and made a mockery of all his promises not to demand anything more from her. He took, insisting on a response, telling her without words what he wanted, how he felt.

The girl he'd once known would have run from this kiss, but the woman he held now might as well have flung out a challenge. She dared him to take what he wanted, urging him with her hands deep in his hair, her tongue dueling with his.

He'd known she could make him want with gut-wrenching desire. He hadn't known he was so close to losing control, that her heat ignited him like a firecracker fuse. His hand edged under her shirt, fingers skimming upward.

"Ahem."

At the interruption, Laura jerked back from his touch, leaving him so hot he felt like a chili pepper stewing in its own juice. It took several deep breaths before he realized his brother Rafe had joined them on the porch.

Rafe, laid-back as always, leaned against a porch post and tipped his hat at Laura. "Thought you ought to hear what we found."

"Or didn't find?" Chase asked, casually slinging one arm over Laura's shoulder.

"You guessed?"

"Dad suspected," Chase admitted, swallowing hard, not wanting the sweet taste of her still on his lips when he lied.

"I called in ten minutes ago."

Rafe's air of absolute casualness warned Chase. The more relaxed Rafe appeared, the deeper his emotions. If Rafe had already spoken to the Senator, he knew how they intended to lie to Laura.

"I don't speak Sutton," Laura said, temper in her voice, banked passion in her eyes as she looked from Chase to Rafe. "What's going on? You did find my tracks?"

"Sorry, ma'am. We found tracks all over, but nary a one from your horse."

"But—"

"The fence wasn't mended like you said, either."

"But that's impossible." Laura trembled with rage and Chase tightened his grip on her shoulder.

He dreaded destroying her, wished he could think of another way to protect Tyler. "It's possible someone arrived ahead of Rafe and the sheriff, hid your tracks and broke the fence."

"There *were* fresh tracks up there. Lots of them." Rafe packed a pipe and fired it up, the pungent tobacco rising into the air. "We should have lit out sooner."

"Is that it?" Chase asked, knowing Rafe knew damn well he hadn't yet told Laura the lie. Because if Chase had, he'd have hardly have been necking with her on the Embry front porch.

Rafe, always sensitive to others, would instinctively know Chase hadn't yet told her. Would he also realize that Chase couldn't bring himself to say the words himself?

In the darkness, the two men exchanged a look. Rafe's eyes asked for permission and forgiveness while shooting out a measure of compassion. Slowly Chase nodded, feeling as if he'd just sealed his own casket.

"I'm sorry." His brother's soft drawl rasped Chase's conscience like a file. "Tyler—"

"How is he?" Laura asked.

"He didn't make it to Denver."

"No!" Laura's voice rose. "He was still breathing when he left. He...he..."

"He's gone. The funeral's set for the day after tomorrow." Rafe took a step forward and lifted Laura's chin, raising her head until their eyes met. "Not everyone in this town believes you're guilty. The Senator and me, included."

Her voice trembled. "I thank you for that."

"But just the same, it might be better if you didn't show at the funeral."

Chapter Six

Despite their best efforts to unearth family secrets, the press hadn't discovered that Tyler was receiving the best medical care available to bring him out of the coma. So while his brother lay unconscious under a false name in a military hospital, Chase had stood stoically through the fake funeral in Highview, wondering if the reporters were hounding Laura back at the Embry ranch.

To know that she was now the number one suspect for the murder of both his brothers left Chase worried and he'd returned to Laura as soon as the phony funeral service ended. He'd shoved past a few reporters at the cemetery but they hadn't followed him onto the Embry ranch, no doubt due to several hands guarding the front gate with shotguns.

He knocked on the Embry's front door. Laura opened the door warily and, after recognizing him, came outside with Keith at her heels, her scent of lemons and rain a balm to his soul. "A few members of the press camped in the front yard yesterday. Since Dad posted guards, it's been better, but I've been careful about going outside."

He hated the hunted look in her eyes and it made

his voice rough as he gestured to the chairs on the porch. "We need to talk."

Oblivious to the tension of the adults, Keith toddled happily to the new swing set his grandparents had installed for him. "Go slide."

Laura settled on the porch swing where she could keep watch of Keith, her gaze avoiding Chase. "Keith, stay where I can see you."

Chase couldn't help noticing that her golden hair set off her satiny skin—skin that he ached to touch.

"Slide fast," their son agreed, his tiny legs pumping at full speed.

Chase watched him go, unable to restrain a proud grin at this marvelous addition to his life. His son was the future. And every day, Keith seemed to grow taller, speak better, move faster. "He seems happy here."

"Who wouldn't be?"

He watched Laura's gaze lovingly take in the open blue skies, breeze-swaying grass and their jubilant son, and wished the moment could continue forever. He couldn't help noting the new worry lines around her eyes, the tension at her mouth. She looked as if she'd lost weight. Guilt that he'd lied to her about Tyler churned in his stomach.

He ached to take her into his arms and kiss away her fears but didn't know if she'd welcome the intimacy. Instead, Chase ignored his swiftly rising pulse, straddled a chair and swung a battered leather briefcase onto his lap. "We have work to do."

"We do?"

"For the past two years, you assumed you killed Brent. Now we know better."

She bit her bottom lip, her characteristic gesture

whenever she was troubled, and smoothed a crease in her jeans with long, slender fingers. From the intensity and hesitation of her expression, he knew she'd been thinking of little else but solving the murder since he'd been gone. "Knowing the truth won't clear me."

"But now that *we* know you are innocent, we can look for whoever killed Brent…and Tyler."

She brushed a wisp of blond hair from blue eyes clouded with worry and focused on him. "You think the same person killed both of them?"

He wanted to tell her not to worry, it was all a mistake he could straighten out and she would be free. But determined to treat her intelligence with the respect she deserved, he wouldn't lie again, instead giving her all the hope he could. "It seems logical to believe one person was after Brent and Tyler. And the Senator believes the killer let the horses loose the night of Tyler's murder to give someone time to obscure your tracks."

Laura's eyes opened wide in pleased surprise. "I thought Rafe was just being kind the other night. The Senator really doesn't think I'm the killer?"

"Let's say he's keeping an open mind."

Her eyes teared. "It's because of Keith, isn't it? He can't stand the thought of the mother of his grandchild being a murderer."

"Maybe." Chase wanted to be as honest with her as possible. He couldn't stomach any more lies. He couldn't stand how much he was hurting her by letting her believe Tyler was dead. "But the Senator also knows you. And he trusts my judgment."

Laura's voice wobbled. "I suppose he didn't become a Senator by trusting the obvious."

"Exactly." Although his gut churned, outwardly Chase ignored her stress, knowing pride kept her from wanting his pity or his sympathy. He snapped open the briefcase and removed a sheaf of papers. "The Senator even gave me the employment records that go back two years."

Laura shook her head. "The murderer might not have been an employee."

"True, but we have to start somewhere. While anyone could have gone to the barn if they meant to do harm, we have to narrow our investigation to the most obvious suspects. I've already crossed off those employees whose work didn't regularly take them to the barn—like the office staff and house-maids. Then I compared the current list of employ-ees to those that worked for Brent two years ago."

"Thank you," she spoke softly. "That must have taken hours."

"I haven't slept much," he admitted, ignoring the weary exhaustion that never seemed to go away. And whenever he closed his eyes, all he saw was Laura's worried blue eyes.

"Would you like some coffee?"

"No, th—"

"Keith!" She jumped to her feet. "Go down the slide *feet* first."

With a mischievous grin, Keith twisted himself around and pointed his feet to the ground. "Okey-dokey."

Laura settled back into her chair with a sigh, her slender fingers tapping her thigh and revealing frayed nerves. "So how many people did you come up with?"

''Too many. Twenty-three. I was hoping you could think of a way to cross some off.''

Chase gave her a list and she scanned it, then let the paper flutter to her lap. ''All I can think of is adding names.''

''What names?''

''Brent and Tyler's girlfriends. Jealous boyfriends. Someone's framing me—so maybe I have an enemy I don't know about. And what about the men playing cards with the Senator the night of Tyler's accident? Judges Stewart and Perkins were there along with my attorney and Mac Nolan the reporter. It's just too many people. How can we narrow the list?''

''We go talk to them. See if they have an alibi.'' The open V of her shirt revealed a golden swatch of silky skin that tempted him to reach out and touch her. Knowing the thought was inappropriate did nothing to still his yen to take her into his arms and he wondered what it was about this woman that captivated him like no other. Was it her combination of softness and strength? He could barely keep his thoughts on the conversation. ''I think we should start with Lance since he was near the stable the night of Brent's death and since he was the first person to find Tyler.''

''The sheriff already questioned him.''

''Most likely he only asked Lance questions about you. We need to find out if anyone else was around.''

Laura remained still, stiff, silent. He could tell she didn't want to argue with him, but she wasn't enthusiastic about his plan, either.

Unable to resist, he reached out and took her icy hand, trying to imbue her with warmth. "What?"

She shrugged. "It's not that I don't appreciate what you're trying to do, but it just seems…hopeless. We aren't trained investigators. Maybe you should turn the records over to the sheriff."

Chase didn't like the unhappy look in her eyes, as if she didn't think the battle worth fighting. If he had to prick her anger to get her moving, he was willing to do it. His voice turned gruff. "Why would the sheriff investigate further? He already thinks you're guilty."

ANGER HAD PROPELLED Laura to accompany Chase over to the Sutton ranch. She felt guilty for leaving her son with her mother since she knew Anna had chores, but she told herself it was important that grandmother and grandson get to know one another better. Still, her mom had a lot to do and Keith would only slow her down. Small ranches like theirs were only a wolf-scratch away from financial ruin and every pair of able hands was necessary to keep them going.

Yet in the magnificence of the unspoiled valley ringed by mountains, with its scent of green grass and sounds of bawling cows, it always seemed there were flickers of miraculous redemption around the next bend. The trick to survival was to keep going. Thanks goodness for Chase who had that determination bred into his very bone marrow. He wouldn't ever give up and he wouldn't let her, either. She took comfort in knowing that no matter what happened, she would never forget how much he believed in her—even without a shred of proof.

They'd ridden horses, cutting through knee-high grass pastures and fording the shallow river to avoid using the road where the press might have the opportunity to confront them. They hadn't spoken much and Laura was content to bask in the warmth of the midday sun, revel in the fine horseflesh beneath her and the even finer man beside her. She wanted to remember every detail of the moment, the determined set of Chase's shoulders, the hard angle of his chin, his gentle hold on the reins as he guided his mount around a crevice.

All too soon, they crossed onto Sutton land and dismounted at the metal building that smelled of concrete and diesel and housed tractors, trucks and other assorted ranching vehicles. They found Lance under a jacked-up truck, changing the oil, only his long-legged jeans and scuffed books sticking out from beneath the engine.

Lance slid from under the truck, holding between gloved hands a tray of dirty oil. This was the first time Laura had seen the mechanic up close and hearing aids in both ears were plainly visible. She'd guess from the leather-deep tan, gray hair and crinkles around his eyes he was fiftyish. Drops of oil spattered his face that wore a surprised but honest expression.

Lance's gaze fixed on Chase first. "Howdy." Then he tipped his hat politely to Laura. "Ma'am."

"Got a minute?" Chase asked in a loud voice, leading Lance away from a group of curious mechanics and toward the back door where the men stepped out to smoke.

"Let me wash up." Lance removed his gloves, headed to a sink and rejoined them a few minutes later. "Now, what can I do for you?"

"We wanted to ask about the night of Brent's murder," Laura said firmly. Determined to do her part, she refused to take a back seat to Chase's investigation. Chase had been right to prod her anger. This was her life and her son that she was fighting for.

Lance pointed to his ear. "Sorry, you'll have to speak up."

Chase repeated Laura's statement and Lance nodded in understanding. "Don't know what I can tell you."

"You were working on a truck that evening," Laura said, trying to remind him of the night in question.

"Yep. The distributor cap was cracked. Had to order a new one. Waited three days for it to come in."

Lance might be hearing impaired but his memory seemed exceptional—at least for all things mechanical. When he pulled a tin of chewing tobacco out of his back pocket, pinched black leaves between his fingers and then stuffed it into his cheek, Laura tried not to let disapproval show on her face. "Who else did you see around the barn that night?"

Lance's brows rose in surprise. "Besides Brent and you?"

She felt compelled to explain. "I only stabbed Brent once in the chest. But the autopsy report showed he died of a second stab wound to the throat. Someone else had to be there that night."

Chase spoke more loudly than usual but kept his

tone even. "We're trying to find out who else was around."

Lance's eyes suddenly rounded with wariness. "I didn't kill him!"

Was his protest too vehement? Had he jumped to that statement because he *was* guilty? Laura wished she was better at reading people. It didn't seem reasonable that Lance would have killed Brent and then hung around another two years and killed Tyler, too. He had no motivation that she was aware of. And yet, did she expect a killer to be reasonable?

Chase laid a calming hand on Lance's shoulder. "If we thought you hurt my brother we wouldn't have come asking you first off."

"We just hoped you might remember someone else," Laura added.

"I don't recollect anyone. I had my head under the truck's hood. I was trying to fix—"

"You saw me," Laura prodded and Chase shot her a look of approval that warmed her to her toes.

Lance crossed his boots at the ankle and leaned against the building, staring off at the horizon. Laura hoped he was trying to remember, but it was just as likely he was enjoying his tobacco, his thoughts miles away.

The mechanic spit and then turned to Chase. "The Senator was playing cards that night. I believe his poker buddies drove by. The two judges, the sheriff and that reporter fella...."

"Mac Nolan?" Chase asked.

"Yeah."

Laura reined in her frustration. These men played poker every Friday night. There was nothing suspicious about them being around. Unless— "Did any of them stop at the barn?"

"I believe one of them had to answer a call of nature."

"Who stopped?"

"Judge Perkins."

"I never saw him," Laura said.

"They went on up to the house before you arrived."

Laura sighed in frustration. If the man had left before she arrived, he couldn't have stabbed Brent. "Well, that's that."

"Are you sure they all went up to the house together?" Chase asked.

Lance scratched his head. "Now, that I think on it, I ain't sure."

They could easily check with the Senator and his other poker buddies to see if anyone had arrived late that night. Suddenly, Laura's hopes raised a notch. Questioning Lance had been an excellent idea and she reminded herself to let Chase know exactly how much she appreciated his helping her. Just knowing that he would never quit on her gave her the courage to go on.

Chase plugged away with more questions. "Okay, what about *after* Laura arrived? Did you see anyone else around?"

"Nope."

"The barn couldn't have been empty. What about the girls who exercise the horses or muck out the stalls?"

"Nope. I didn't see nobody between the judge entering the side door and Laura leaving that way—"

"That's it!" Excitement shot through Laura like a spark about to ignite a fuse. "I didn't leave through the side door."

"You didn't?" Chase asked.

"I went in through the side door. But I ran out the front."

Laura turned to Lance more hopeful than she'd been in weeks. "Can you describe the person you saw?"

"It was dark. I assumed it was you."

"Why did you assume that?" Chase asked modulating his tone, but she could still hear the enthusiasm lying beneath the surface.

"Well, I saw Miss Embry go in. I just figured it was her coming out. You have to understand, I wasn't paying no never mind to her. I was working."

"I understand, Lance." Laura praised him, hoping he might recall some other detail. "You've been very helpful."

"Please think," Chase urged. "This is real important. What made you think the person you saw was Laura? Was it height? Weight? Hair color?"

Lance shook his head. "It was too dark for details. But now that I think on it, it was the way she moved or rather the way a black shadow moves against a gray background. I'd swear those were female hips swaying. You know what I mean?"

Laura recalled the long stand of blond hair found near Tyler in the barn. The only woman in these parts who had hair close to the same color as hers was the sheriff's dispatcher. "Could it have been Francesca Martin you saw that night?"

"Could have been any female. It was dark."

"You could have recognized Francesca in the daytime?" Chase asked.

"I suppose."

But from Chase's list of employees, Laura knew that Francesca hadn't worked on the Sutton ranch when Brent had died. "How did you know Francesca?"

"Her mama works in the Sutton kitchen. We used to be close."

"Francesca lives with her mother on the ranch?"

Lance shook his head. "Not anymore. I believe she's the sheriff's dispatcher."

They questioned Lance for another thirty minutes but he'd given them everything he could remember. Laura thought through the information and looked over her shoulder at Chase on the ride back to the Embry ranch. "I need to speak to Bradley face-to-face about what we've found out. Maybe tell the sheriff, too, but I dread going into town."

"Because of the press."

"That mostly. And right now, I don't feel like running into any old friends." She really just wanted to hide with her baby in her arms and Chase at her side. She shoved the image away. If going into town was necessary to find the person who had set her up, she would do so.

With the new information, they could cut Chase's list of suspects way down. Not that many women worked on the ranch. If they could limit their suspects to females who had access to the barn, the task of finding the murderer might be possible. She put Francesca Martin at the top of her list. The thought of another woman setting her up for murder made Laura angry enough to quit thinking about hiding.

Anger she'd long submerged bubbled to the surface, fueling her for the battle to come.

No one would take away her life. Not without a damn good fight.

"YOU SURE YOU want to drive into Highview?" Chase asked Laura as they waved goodbye to Keith and Anna Embry. He didn't like seeing Laura under so much pressure, flinched at the pain he saw in her. He felt as if her pain were part of him, a razor of agony slicing through him whenever he thought of how much she loved their son, how she might lose him forever if she went to jail.

After giving Chase a brittle smile that was all edges and no real warmth, she leaned her head back on the seat and closed her eyes. "I spoke to Bradley on the phone. He'll have the sheriff waiting so we'll only have to tell them Lance's story once."

Chase was perceptive enough to realize that she didn't want to go back to the county jail and he didn't blame her.

He would have liked to have saved her the agony of going into town at all, but maybe some good would come of it. They could talk to Francesca after they finished with the attorney and sheriff. He also wanted to question Judge Perkins. Even if his father couldn't recall if Judge Perkins had been late to the game that night, maybe he'd seen someone in the barn—someone like Francesca Martin. And according to his father's records, Sally Walker, Bradley's secretary had been working for the Suttons two years ago on the day of Brent's death, so she also was someone who'd had means and opportunity. Although Sally had long since given up working with

horses, Chase wanted to ask her what she'd seen that
night. He planned to gather all the information he
could before he confronted the people who had been
at the Sutton barn during both Brent's murder and
Tyler's accident.

"We still don't have any solid proof, you know,"
Laura reminded him, pulling him from his thoughts.
She looked good just sitting in the front of his
pickup, her skirt riding up her knee, high enough for
him to see she hadn't bothered with stockings. Not
that she needed them over her lean, tanned legs.
"My fingerprints are the only ones on the pitchfork."

Chase hadn't figured out who had killed one
brother and put the other in a coma yet, but his heart
told him it wasn't Laura. It couldn't be because
every time he considered it, his stomach hitched at
the thought. And a third part of his anatomy had a
mind all its own and was stirring in his jeans just
from the slightest encouragement from her. To distract himself, he forced his thoughts back to the
problem. "The sheriff will have to consider Lance
a credible witness. At least he can verify that someone else was there that night."

"Not necessarily." Laura looked at him with
wide, dark eyes. "We only have my word which
door I exited."

Chase's fingers tightened around the steering
wheel. "The sheriff *will* reopen his investigation.
And we've just begun to dig into the past. There's
no telling what Francesca, Sally or Judge Perkins
can tell us." Chase squinted as he drove around a
mountain bend, the sun a blazing yellow orb shining
in his eyes. He reached for his sunglasses that he

kept above the visor. "Oh, I almost forget to tell you. The Senator called. Lance may not be the sterling character we thought."

"What do you mean?" She rubbed the bend in her neck and he thought of nuzzling her there.

Keep your eyes on the road, your mind where it belongs, he told himself. "Dad said that Brent wanted to fire Lance."

"What for?" She twisted in her seat and the air conditioner picked up her scent of lemon and rain and shot it his way.

He had difficulty keeping the huskiness out of his tone. "Brent claimed the man was sneaky."

"Sneaky?"

If she didn't stop chewing her bottom lip, he wasn't going to be accountable for his actions. What made his situation even more difficult was the fact that she had absolutely no idea how she effected him. Swallowing a grunt of dissatisfaction over his inability to control his wandering thoughts, he forced his voice to stay calm. "Apparently, Brent didn't like the way Lance stared at him."

"But he watches people's lips because he doesn't hear well. Lip movements help him figure out our words."

Chase shrugged, hoping to ease the tension between his shoulder blades and elsewhere. "That's what I always thought. But now we can cast doubt on your guilt. Lance had opportunity, means and motive."

"What motive?" she asked.

"Maybe he thought Brent was about to fire him, but that's a weak motive for murder."

"It's still my prints on—"

"Did Lance wear gloves that night like the ones he had on the other day?"

Her forehead scrunched into cute lines as she thought hard. Finally she shook her head. "I don't remember."

"Keep thinking. Maybe it'll come back to you."

Sun glared in his eyes and a puff of dust popped off the road and swirled like a miniature tornado. Chase stared hard at the spot and pointed. "You see that?"

"What?"

Before he could answer her, something pinged and sparked off the truck's hood.

"Someone's shooting at us!" He jerked the wheel hard to the right and then the left, fishtailing the vehicle.

"I didn't hear any shots."

"Maybe the shooter is too far away. Maybe they have a silencer."

Laura craned her neck, looking for the shooter. "Are you sure?"

"Keep your head down. Tighten your seat belt. We're going off the road."

"But—"

"Hold on!"

He spun the tires and veered onto an old cattle trail, hoping trees would provide cover. The truck bounced hard, sideswiped a tree and teetered.

Laura screamed, "We're going over."

"No, we're not!"

He fought the truck like a bucking bronco and brought it down on all four tires. Thankful the engine kept purring, he jammed the pedal to the metal, steering around boulders, stray pines and old fence posts.

At the sight of the swollen creek, he slammed on his brakes, screamed to a stop in a roar of dust.

Laura reached into her purse and yanked out her cell phone. "I'll call for help."

From a distance the trees had appeared thick enough to hide behind, but up close she could see they were spaced too sparsely to provide good cover. The shooter had them pinned down and might kill them before the sheriff arrived. They'd have to save themselves. Still, help on the way couldn't hurt. While Laura phoned, he surveyed the creek.

In late summer the mountain runoff would slow to a trickle, but right now the icy water surged swift and sure, flooding its banks with a fury. White water swirled around sunken rocks and a few logs bounced, caught in the cascading surge. Swimming across the stream would be impossible. He opened his door, intending to test the water's depth on foot before blindly driving forward, when another shot pinged off a rock beside him.

The bullet bounced off a rock, ricocheted, cracked the windshield, leaving a spiderweb of splinters and Laura ducking below the dash.

He rammed the truck into gear. "You okay?"

"Just peachy."

She wouldn't be for long if they didn't get out of there. The shooter, hidden in the mountains above them, would pick them off like tin cans sitting on a fence post. If they didn't move, they'd be shot so full of holes, they wouldn't even float in brine. Hemmed in by boulders large enough to trap the truck but not big enough to provide cover, he had no room to maneuver. Backing up the truck slowly was out of the question. So was running on foot.

Laura's face paled with fear. "The phone system is busy. A recording suggests we try again in ten minutes."

Chase eased off the gas and splashed the truck into the rushing creek. "We don't have ten minutes."

Chapter Seven

Laura pressed her feet against the floorboards and rammed her back against the truck's seat. With her right hand she gripped the door handle, wedging herself in as best she could, ignoring the hot and cold coils of fear that washed through her. With bullets spitting out of the sky like hail in a summer storm, she'd had no chance to refasten her seat belt before water flooded the floorboards.

Gushing water caught the side of the truck, spinning them sideways, hurling them downstream. The engine sputtered and coughed but didn't die.

"How long will the truck float?"

Face intense with concentration, Chase shifted into four-wheel drive, the muscles in his forearms cording with effort. "Not long enough to make it to the other side. We need to find some shallows."

The truck slammed into creek bottom and tires caught on silt, river gravel and rock, snaring them at a cockeyed position. Chase worked the gas pedal, using the current to angle them toward the far bank. The truck rocked, gears churned, and water rushed inside the cab.

She shouted over the rushing water that turned her feet to ice. "Now what?"

"Hang on!"

Chase gunned the engine, a tire caught. The truck lurched forward and then they were bumping and grinding across the creek and finally back onto solid ground. Chilled to her core, Laura craned her neck, looking for the shooter as the sun glared mockingly in her eyes.

Chase caught sight of her peering out the window, uncoiled his arm and dragged her across the seat. "Keep your head down."

She slid closer to him just as another bullet thwacked harmlessly into the seat where she'd been just moments before.

Chase drove like a madman with one hand, while his other cradled her head against his chest. "Just hang on, honey."

"I'm not going anywhere." She clung to him, very glad he'd insisted on coming with her into town this afternoon. Burrowing her cheek against his hard warmth, molding herself to his chiseled chest, she closed her eyes and made herself draw a deep breath. She listened for the sounds of shots hitting the truck but could hear nothing beyond the steady beat of Chase's heart.

Water slowly drained out of the cab, leaving behind soggy carpet, water dripping off the inside of the windows and steam rising off the engine's hood. Chase turned the heater to high and didn't slow down until he'd rounded a curve, out of the line of fire. "Why don't you try calling the sheriff again."

His words took seconds to penetrate through the current of warmth that curled around her like a blanket. She had to force herself to leave his side and search for her purse that had fallen to the floor.

Pulling the soggy bag next to her, she rooted inside without much hope. "Got it." She tried to turn on the power but the batteries didn't light up. She'd been so busy clinging to him, she'd forgotten to protect the one thing that might save them. Anger at herself mixed with regret and left her feeling numb. She spoke through chattering teeth. "The phone's dead. I'm sorry, I shouldn't have let it get wet."

"It's not your fault. Even Super Woman couldn't have held on through all that bouncing."

"Where's your phone?"

He grinned sheepishly. "I left it in the charger. But we're safe enough now. If the shooter's on foot it'll take hours to walk down the mountain."

"And if he has a vehicle?"

"He'd have to take the same route we did."

At the unlikeliness of anyone following their madcap dash through the swollen creek, dangerous tension flowed out of her to be replaced by a new kind. Chase reached out to her and she snuggled against his side, remembering the bullets clipping rocks just inches from his head, realizing how close she'd come to losing him. Too damned close. She didn't know if she could stand to be separated from him again, feel again the black and endless loneliness enshrouding her, freezing her, all the way to her soul.

Chase stroked her shoulder, his fingers swirling a path of heat over her icy flesh. "I'm betting the shooter will expect us to head to town, so we'll hide out here until dark."

"Hide where?"

"Somewhere I can warm you."

The tenderness in his eyes, the huskiness in his voice and his fingers now caressing her scalp told her he wanted her. He'd just saved their lives, why not trust her body to his keeping? While the last two years had left her starving for his touch, the past few minutes had made her very aware how short these hours together might be.

"It may take a long time to warm me up." She stretched, deliberately arching her back and letting her wet clinging shirt emphasize her curves and wasn't disappointed as his eyes flared into smoke and cinders.

"Is that so?" The pulse in a vein at his throat beat irregularly as he hurriedly steered through a tall stand of pine and jerked the truck to a stop. Effectively hidden from the shooter's original location, he switched off the engine and then drew her so close she could see the steel of his irises mirroring her own hunger.

He twined his fingers into her hair and she breathed in the scent of man, soap and coffee as he brushed his mouth against hers. "Laura…" He said her name with a sigh, a breath, a question. "Look at me," he dared gently.

She met his challenge and the need she saw burning in the depths of his eyes made her breath go ragged as desire spiraled heat straight to her core. The past washed away on a tidal wave. The future lay murky in fog. But the present thundered in her ears. She would have spoken of the lightning sizzling inside her but all she could do was reach up and draw his mouth to hers.

His freshly shaved jaw teased her palms, taunting

her with a need to touch him all over. She ached to draw him closer, envelop herself in his heat, explore by touch and taste every bared inch of flesh that he offered. She'd spent two long years wondering whether this moment would ever come to be, dreaming of his muscular arms wrapping her in an embrace and creating magical moments. She wanted to hang on to time and never let go and as if reading her mind, he moved slowly, letting her enjoy his quiet scent, his whispery touch, his clenching heat.

With one finger, he traced her mouth, and her lips parted in surprise at the intimacy of his gesture. She leaned into him, silently asking for more and he accepted her invitation to lightly explore her front teeth with the pad of his finger. She nipped lightly, threaded her hands into his dark, silky hair and tugged him closer.

He gave her more, but only his mouth. But what a mouth—ultra X-rated and sensual. She never knew a kiss could be so sweet and yet so tauntingly, temptingly erotic. Slowly his tongue parted her mouth, exploring, nibbling, questing and she forgot everything but her lips, shocked that her being was reduced to his next mind-altering caress.

He drew back and murmured into her ear, ''Warming up?''

''Only a little.'' She threw her hands around his neck and cocked her brow. ''I thought you said something about making me warm. All over.''

He let out a low whistle. ''Girls who like to play with fire get burned.''

She wouldn't risk another pregnancy, not until she cleared her name. Not until she and Chase discussed the future. However the last two years had been so hard, she'd learned to take good times where she could find them.

Tilting her head back, she looked directly into his eyes. "This *woman's* on the pill."

"I see."

But Chase obviously had questions in his eyes and she'd never been one to play games. She set his mind at ease. "Doctor's order to regulate my cycle."

"You know I'm jealous as hell of anything that touches you, even your clothes. Especially your clothes." A wide grin lit up his face and when her face heated, he chuckled with quiet pleasure. "But I don't want that luscious skin marred by pine needles. So," he opened his truck door, slid out of the seat and lifted the lid of his toolbox, "let's see if the emergency provisions are still dry."

Many ranchers kept a first-aid kit, a compass, flares and matches handy. Some kept guns, water and blankets—perhaps even a fishing line and hook in their vehicles. Even in the days of cell phones, it could be hours before help arrived and in winter, staying warm for hours could make the difference in whether a stranded cowpoke survived.

On a balmy summer day like this one, there was no chance of hypothermia setting in. Still she was happy to see the dry blanket Chase kept in the toolbox that spanned the width of the truck bed. Moments later, he'd spread the blanket on a bed of pine needles.

And suddenly her mouth went dry.

Show time!

Chase hadn't ever seen her wearing nothing but sunlight. Before, they'd always made love in the dark. He hadn't seen what nine months of pregnancy and breast feeding had done to her body. Not that she had ever been perfect. Her hips were wider than she'd have liked and her thighs were no longer muscle-tight from hours in the saddle.

"Nervous?" Chase asked.

Indignant that he could read her vulnerability so easily, she placed her hands on her hips. "How'd you know?"

"You were chewing on your lip again."

"Oh." Her stomach clenched with nervousness. "Perhaps this isn't such a good idea. Suppose the shooter finds us?"

"Not even Tarzan could swim across that creek." He kicked off shoes and socks, then unbuttoned the top button of his denim shirt drawing attention to a yummy bronze expanse of skin dusted with fine black hairs that curled into crisp spirals. When he notice her fascination, he undid one shirt button after another, slowly, stripping with an easy sensuality that made her stomach lurch into her throat.

When his jeans interfered with unfastening the last buttons, he yanked his tucked-in shirt from his jeans and peeled it off, revealing shoulders wide as the Rocky Mountains and hard as granite that tapered to a waist of flat abs and hip-hugging denim. She sucked in her breath at the bulge in his jeans, pleased he so obviously wanted her.

As if he hadn't a hurry in the world, Chase hung his shirt over a low tree branch, all without turning away from her. "Look at me, Laura. I can't deny how much I want you." Long tapered fingers unfastened the top snap on his low-slung jeans and fingered the next. "But the choice is yours. I'll stop right now if…"

When she remained silent, his brows raised, waiting for her reply. She couldn't speak. She couldn't move. Through pine-bough filtered sunlight, he locked his gaze on her face, his intensity focused, his confidence in his desire and hers gleaming through the dust motes. He unfastened the last three buttons, revealing navy cotton boxers.

Calmly, he hung his jeans next to his shirt and turned back to her. They stood less than six feet apart, but she swore she could feel fire radiating off his flesh. He hooked his thumbs into the boxers.

Blood roared in her ears. "Don't stop now."

In one swift graceful movement, he stood naked and she sucked in her breath at the magnificent male standing before her. He reminded her of a proud jungle cat, all muscle, taut sinews and hewed bone.

"I'm not as pretty as you are." To her own ears, her voice sounded like a stranger's.

At her compliment, Chase's eyes twinkled with merriment and need. "Darling, to turn me on, all you have to do…is be here."

All doubts, all hesitancy vanished with his words. And with a boldness that rose from her core, she found the courage to match his magnificence. "I can do better than just show up. Wait right there."

"You're leaving me standing here wearing nothing but an erection?" Laughter warmed his protest.

She raised her eyebrows up and down in an exaggerated leer. "I like your outfit. It's classic. And it'll never go out of style."

"Then your wish is my command," he told her, but she heard him growl something under his breath about her not taking too long which she pretended not to hear.

She didn't go far. Just to the truck to switch on the key and flick the radio to Highview's country station. She returned to him with her hips swaying to Reba's latest love song and with a shimmy she kicked off one shoe and then the other. Stepping onto the blanket, she danced for him, slowly lifting her shirt over her head, revealing just an inch of flesh at her waist and then a little more.

His muscles strained from the taut lines at his neck to the lean lines of his tensing calves. Every muscle looked constricted and ready to pounce and she guessed only his dominant will kept him from reaching for her.

The glint in his eyes that never left her for a second made her bold, made her carefree and eager to give him an afternoon he'd never forget. Eventually she showed him her lacy taupe bra and then twirled her shirt over her head, letting loose a sigh of satisfaction when it actually landed on the pine branches next to his.

Chase didn't turn his head to see where her skirt landed. He was too busy devouring her with his eyes. She sashayed out of her skirt and almost lost her nerve. Spinning around, she gave him her back before taking off her bra.

"Please, Laura," he said, his voice hoarse. "Come to me."

When she turned back to him, she'd strategically crossed her hands over her breasts.

"You little tease." Chase lunged, tackled her, twisted in the air and then broke her fall with his big body as they laughingly fell to the blanket.

She landed on top of him and admired the play of light dappling his bronzed flesh, emphasizing the hollows and lines of his muscular torso, his dark hair catching ripples of sunshine. His fingers massaged her back, shooting tiny arcs of sizzle down her spine.

She cupped his jaw. "I've missed you."

"I want you so damn bad I'm ready to burst." With a soft groan, he captured her lips and pulled her mouth to his, giving much more than he took. She swirled her fingers through the satiny whorls of hair at his chest, playfully caressing rippling muscles full of heat.

He murmured with a raspy drawl, "Just hold me a minute. Just hold me. I want this to be sweet for both of us."

At his soft whisper, she shivered, not from cold but longing. His arms curled around her, his large hands settling on her hips and she wriggled free of her panties. When he let out a broken sigh in her ear, then she knew he had missed her as much as she'd missed him. The rightness of holding him burned through her like fine cognac, potent and powerful and swift, heating her with a fire that freed her from the icy loneliness of the past two years.

Laura parted her legs, drew her knees up under her until she straddled him and found Chase waiting for her, letting her make the first moves. She trailed her hair over him as she rose to her knees, easing herself over him, taking his heat and his hardness and his belief in her straight to her heart.

He let out an incoherent groan of pleasure that fueled her senses. As her hips rocked, she had to force herself to move slowly, drawing out their enjoyment. Until she could wait no more.

Restraining her impatience, Chase's hands slid from her waist to her rib cage to her breasts, trapping her in a web of sensual caresses. "Hold still."

"I can't."

"Sure you can."

His magical fingers flickered over heightened nerve endings and she bucked wildly, urging him to hasten the pace, move deeper, stronger, faster. Single-mindedly, he refused to be hurried, closed his fingers over her breasts creating a delightful symphony of music that sang through each tender nerve ending until she bit her lip to keep from crying out with joy.

She savored the experience, enchanted by his body, enthralled by his focus on her, as if she were the only woman he'd ever touched, as if she were the only woman in creation. At that moment, the rest of the world ceased to exist. She felt only what he wanted her to feel, heard only his words, tasted only his salty flesh.

He moved suddenly, reversing their positions until she lay on her back, looking skyward. With a predatory gleam in his eyes he took her mouth again, his hips moving with exquisite slowness. He spoke softly, feathering tiny, exquisite nips down her neck. "I've dreamed of you and me...like this.... We're good together."

She groaned. "Actually, I think we're bad together. I want you too much."

"Slow down, woman. I'm not finished with you, yet." He slipped his hand between them and she curved into the waves of pleasure. At the same time, his mouth closed over the tip of her breast, teeth closing around her hardened nipple.

"Oh, my." She arched her back at the wet heat, her hips rising to meet him as waves of pleasure short-circuited her senses. She dug her nails into his shoulders. "Don't stop."

"Yes. Laura, yes."

And then with a hoarse male cry, he increased the tempo of his hips, taking everything she offered, making her forget everything except a raw, erotic urgency that took her captive. He thrust deeply one last time, shuddered and sent her soaring to a jubilant freedom she'd never known.

Minutes later she still hadn't regained her breath, hadn't recovered from the marvelous sensation of losing herself. She stared up at the sky, running her fingers over Chase's back, reluctant to release him, wishing she could remain in this peaceful state of bliss.

The moment was so perfect she didn't want to spoil it by talking, didn't have the energy to move. Laura let her mind drift with the scudding cirrus clouds in the blue Colorado sky and held tight to Chase's shoulders.

Eventually he lifted his head, his eyes heavy lidded and sated looking. "Warm enough?"

"Mm."

"Am I too heavy for you?"

"Mm."

He shot her a mischievous grin. "Want to do it again?"

"Mm." With tremendous effort she refocused her gaze from the sky to his face, cupped his cheeks between her hands and locked gazes with him. "I'm so glad I decided to trust you."

At her words, he pulled back with a frown, surprising her. He'd been so loving, so warm and so understanding of her needs but now it was as if her words had doused ice water over a sleeping bear. Perhaps she shouldn't have even referred to her past mistakes but the words needed saying and what better time to tell him how her feelings had deepened?

She trusted herself to make the right decision. And therefore she'd held nothing back.

But oddly, he seemed unwilling to reciprocate. His face had shut down of all expression, alarming her. Surely he wouldn't have made love to her if he was unable to forgive her for running away and keeping Keith's presence a secret?

Perhaps she was mistaken and before doubts started to crowd her thoughts, she figured she'd better come right out and ask. "What's wrong?"

"Nothing."

She shoved him off her chest and rolled onto her side, puzzled by his complete change of mood and attitude. One moment he'd been an insatiable lover and the next, he'd turned into a recalcitrant stranger.

She took his hand and squeezed, willing him to confide in her. "Tell me."

"I can't."

"Can't? Don't you mean *won't?*" At his frosty expression, she shivered, an eerie prickle going down her back that had nothing to do with his physical withdrawal. She refused to believe he'd made love to her out of mere physical need. His feelings for her had been so obvious, she couldn't possibly have been mistaken.

Or had she read him all wrong?

She'd believed his every caress, his tender determination to please her had been the actions of love words still left unsaid. She might not be very experienced but she fully believed Chase had spoken to her with his body, ferociously and fervently.

Chase was silent a long time and she didn't say another word, knew he could see the hurt in her eyes. When he finally spoke, he barely sounded like himself. His eyes were bleak, his tone pure steel. "I gave my word to keep a secret and I can't go back on my promise."

WITH HIS CLOTHES mostly dry and the setting sun long behind the mountains, Chase backed the truck out from the pines that had hidden them from any prying eyes. The afternoon had been spent in long awkward silences and he could have kicked himself like a stupid mule for being unable to let Laura's comment about trust fall by the wayside.

But how could he forget the monumental lie that stood between them? He'd been furious that Laura hadn't trusted him enough to come to him after Brent's death and now that she did trust him, he wasn't worthy of her trust.

In addition to being charged with Brent's murder, she now had the additional pressure of waiting to be charged with a second homicide. The one moment where she finally relaxed and turned to him, he'd let her down. He must have been in the basement when they handed out brains. While he wouldn't break his promise to the Senator, he should have just ignored Laura's comment and made love to her again.

Making love to her had been so satisfying he

hadn't been thinking straight. He'd reacted emotion-
ally, from the heart, hating that he'd been the one
to serve her up with the blackest of betrayals. And
not only had he spoiled their afternoon together,
he'd hurt Laura deeply. He'd seen the pain slam into
her, known that only words could fix her pain—
words he couldn't say.

The truck went around a bend and the headlights
picked up little white caps in the swiftly running
waters of the creek. Chase drove along the bank,
using the waterway to guide him.

Laura interrupted his dark thoughts with her first
spoken words in hours. "Do we have to cross the
swollen creek again?" She shivered and rubbed her
arms as if remembering how cold the mountain runoff had been.

He shrugged, realized she couldn't see him in the
dark and cleared his throat. "That depends. I want
to try to head over to the train track. If we can find
it, I'll drive over the same bridge the train uses."

Beside him, Laura gasped. "That track is as narrow as my double bed and a good fifty feet above
the creek."

"More like seventy."

"I'd rather chance the river again."

"The track's not so bad. It's exactly wide enough
for the truck tires to ride on the track. And we won't
get wet."

"I don't mind getting wet. Really. Please, Chase,
let's go back to the river. We crossed once, we can
do it again."

"It's not the wet and cold that I'm worried about.
If we go for the river in the dark, I won't be able

to avoid the big boulders, even if my headlights stay on.''

Laura's voice was tight with strain, one of the reasons he'd avoided telling her how they would drive out. "Keith can't lose both of us.''

"He won't. Tyler, Rafe, me and even Cam, all have driven over that bridge. The trick is not to look down.''

"Damn it, Chase. You knew all afternoon that once it turned dark, we'd have no choice but to do it your way.''

"Yeah.''

"You should have said something.''

"I had other things on my mind.''

Oops. Why did God give him enough sense to want this woman and not enough smarts to keep her happy with him?

He steered around a crevice, lost sight of the river but headed back. If he navigated correctly, he expected to meet up with the train track in about an hour. Night driving through unbroken trails had to be done slow and easy. They'd had enough excitement for one day. He didn't need a broken axle, too.

"I can picture you, Rafe and Tyler up here, but Cameron? He doesn't seem the daredevil type.''

"Cam isn't.'' Chase wanted to kiss her for changing the topic, but then he always wanted to kiss her and didn't need excuses. The woman must have the most kissable lips in Colorado. Once again, he damned himself for wasting the rest of their afternoon.

"As I recall, it was late on a Friday night and Brent had disappeared with a girl. Tyler, Rafe and I were playing poker and drinking the beer the Senator keeps on hand for guests while Cam was reading some science fiction book.'' He grinned at how he used to tease Cam about those books, but his younger brother had been determined to educate himself about poetry, politics, science and space. All that learning and he'd gone on to be a doctor.

''And?'' Laura prodded.

''We were playing Gut. The pot had gotten high as a week's wages and Rafe ran out of money but was holding a killer hand. He told us if he lost, he'd drive his truck over the train's bridge.''

''And?''

''Tyler refused the bet. He wanted cash. The argument escalated, Rafe and Tyler started wrestling across the table, tipping over the cards, the chips and the drinks. Course it wasn't really a fair fight with Tyler being bigger and having more meat on his bones, but Rafe was wiry strong and harder to hold than a greased eel.''

''I thought Suttons always stick together.''

''We do against outsiders, but at home…well, boys will be boys. Anyway, when Rafe and Tyler rolled into Cam—''

''Where were you during the commotion?''

''Me?''

''Yes, and don't sound so innocent. I'm sure you were involved in the fray.''

''Well, I was cheering them on.''

''Which one?''

''Whoever was losing, of course.''

She let out a slow sigh but he could hear the smile behind it. ''Okay, so they rolled into Cam and…?''

''Knocked over his reading lamp. He looked up—''

"He was reading while you cheered your brothers to cream each other?"

"Cam has remarkable powers of concentration. We once dared him to read a page while riding a bronco and he did it."

"Must have been a pretty tame bronco."

"It was, until Brent lit off a firecracker."

"Good Lord, the Senator must have had his hands full with the five of you."

Only four now. But for once he kept his mouth shut. Instead he continued, "Cam was annoyed by the interruption of his reading—must have been a damn good book. You could always tell when he was about to erupt, because unlike the rest of us who shouted and used our fists, he'd turn still and quiet when he was maddest, that giant brain of his switching into high gear. That book, must have been powerfully interesting because Cam reached down, lifted Rafe off Tyler and drew Tyler up by his shirtfront. He was about to knock their sorry heads together—" he paused for effect "—but I saved them."

"You?"

"Yep. I suggested they both drive over the bridge."

"You didn't?"

"Rafe and Tyler glared at each and agreed. Cam wasn't about to go bash their heads in before they tried such a stunt so he let them go."

"But you said Cam drove over this track, too?"

"I'm getting to that part. Cam thought they had more sense and would chicken out so he went along to tease them. Tyler drove first since he was the oldest and he already had his driver's license. When he made it with no problem, Rafe drove back to the other side.'' Chase smiled at the memory. ''Rafe wasn't quite tall enough to reach the brake pedal and see over the steering wheel so he had to lean out the door to see the track.''

''Good, Lord! How old was he?''

''Fourteen.''

''Oh, God. And my son inherited these genes?''

Chase chuckled. ''Rafe always had the balance of a monkey and the timing of a gymnast. Once he made it over, he challenged me to drive it, too.''

''And you had to accept?''

''Sure as cockleburs on a coyote, I wasn't about to let my younger brother best me.''

''And then you dared Cam,'' Laura guessed. ''It's amazing you all made it through adolescence.''

With the terrain steepening, Rafe shifted into four-wheel drive. ''Now you have it. So you see, there's nothing to worry about.''

''But what if a train comes?''

He shot her a rakish grin. ''Well, sometimes, darling, one has to be a bit lucky in life.''

Chapter Eight

Laura squeezed her eyes shut tight but the picture of the thin railroad bridge over the inky chasm remained in her mind, vivid and nightmarish. As Chase swung onto the tracks, his truck bucked like an ornery bull. Her eyes flew open and she let out a gasp.

"Take it easy." Chase didn't turn his head, concentrating on the twin rails that gleamed under his headlights like the path to hell, dark, dangerous and deadly.

"Just because you couldn't hear a train coming doesn't mean that—"

"It's an old Indian trick. Sound carries underground or through steel for miles."

"From how far away?"

He'd stopped, put his ear to the track and listened for the rumble of an oncoming train before he'd driven onto the rails, but she wondered if she was making a mistake to trust his judgment, to trust him. She didn't like the secret between them that made her doubt every thought and feeling.

"We'll be okay."

While she appreciated his attempt to reassure her

and the steadiness of his hands on the wheel, she peered uneasily ahead into a vast tunnel of darkness, her fingers clenched into fists. "Trains come through this way at sixty miles per hour."

"Even if I miscalculated, I have a backup plan."

Her gut twisted into severe knots. "Why do I have the feeling I won't like it?"

"In an emergency, we'll exit the truck and hang under the tracks from the trusses."

"I don't think so." He sounded as if he were planning a spring roundup, crisp, composed and casual, as if he had nerves of granite. She shuddered as she envisioned the train crashing into the empty truck while they hung from a truss by their fingertips, slipping and plunging to the rocks below.

"It won't come to that. We're almost halfway across."

"How can you tell?"

"By the bridge's structural engineering." He kept talking soothingly, the truck rattling from one cross tie to the next while she fought down her bumping pulse, sweaty palms and a crick in her neck from holding herself rigid. One jolt in the wrong direction and it wouldn't make any difference if a train raced by—they'd be long dead.

Ten minutes later Chase swung off the tracks and she heaved a huge sigh of relief. They'd made it! She expected to feel exhilarated that they'd cheated death but weary exhaustion had her fighting to keep her eyes open as Chase swerved around a bend and onto a road.

She must have fallen asleep because when she next opened her eyes, Chase had pulled into a driveway in front of a residence she didn't recognize. "Where are we?"

Chase switched off the engine. "Mark Bradley's house. I figure we need to talk to your attorney about what happened today."

Before Chase shut off the headlights, she glimpsed Bradley's modest ranch home in need of a fresh coat of paint and minor carpentry repairs. A broken shutter swayed with an eerie creak while light shined through a picture window. Laura hoped they wouldn't be waking the man—it was bad enough they were turning up uninvited.

Laura checked her watch. Ten o'clock. Late, but nowhere near the middle of the night. "Let's knock softly and if he doesn't answer come back tomorrow."

Knocking became unnecessary as a huge German sheppard picked up their scent and started barking. Bradley opened the front door, holding the dog by the collar with one hand, a revolver in the other.

Chase moved between Bradley and Laura, protecting her with his body. "It's Chase Sutton and Laura Embry."

Chase might be keeping secrets, but she could not deny his feelings for her—not when he was willing to take a bullet to protect her. With so much to worry about, Laura had to admit that her decision to trust Chase was a good one. As much as she hated uncertainties, she'd just have to assume that his secret was in her best interests.

Bradley put the weapon down on a table and hushed the dog with a soft command. Then he stepped back and gestured for them to enter. "Come on in."

Chase took her hand, walked beside her to the front door and wiped his boots on the mat before entering the foyer. "We had a little trouble meeting with you in town."

"What happened?"

"Someone shot at us," Laura blurted, glad that Chase was touching her. She liked the strength in his fingers, needed his moral support after what they'd gone through together.

They followed Bradley into his home office which was surprisingly comfortable after the shabby exterior. The dog curled up in front of a massive stone fireplace on a braided rug. While Bradley stepped to a sideboard and fixed drinks, Laura took in the pictures of Bradley's family that hung on the walls, a pretty wife, a handsome son and a baby girl swaddled in pink. Everyone in town knew of the horrible automobile accident that had killed his wife and kids in a rain-slick storm. Twenty years later, Bradley still hadn't remarried and obviously, the pictures meant a great deal to him since he surrounded himself with his family's presence. She hated to think he'd never recovered from the tragedy.

Laura accepted a cold cola and Chase a beer. Settling by the fire with a cognac, the heavyset Bradley ignored his desk and the files piled atop it. Clearly, he'd been working and Laura found it sad that only work filled his life. Then she spied a picture of Bradley and his secretary Sally in a casual pose at the office. Maybe Bradley didn't spend all his time alone.

"Tell me what happened," Bradley suggested. "Start at the beginning and tell me everything you can remember. Details can be important."

An hour later after they'd repeated their conversation with Lance and the terrifying episode on the way into town, Bradley swirled the last sip of cognac in his glass. ''You can't identify the shooter?''

Chase shook his head.

''Sounds like you were ambushed.'' He frowned at Chase. ''Who knew you were coming into town to talk with me and the sheriff about what Lance told you?''

''Lance must have suspected,'' Chase said.

Laura thought back to their discussion and the interested faces of the other Sutton mechanics. ''There's no guessing who Lance spoke to or what he said to them after we left. Besides my parents, you and the sheriff knew our destination, and likely your secretary Sally and the sheriff's dispatcher Francesca, too.''

Suddenly, a suspicion popped into her head. Bradley's secretary had worked at the Sutton ranch during the time of Brent's death. While the woman held a job in town during the time of Tyler's accident, the possibilities were too unusual to ignore.

Both the sheriff's dispatcher and Bradley's secretary must have known they were coming into town. Laura frowned, unwilling to accuse the woman or offend her employer with outrageous suspicions. ''What time did you close the office today?'' she asked Bradley.

''I was in court until three. Why?''

''I'm just trying to fix the sequence of events in my head, who knew what and when.''

''What time does Sally close the office?'' Chase asked.

"Around five o'clock." Bradley arched an eyebrow. "What time were you shot at?"

Laura had to give the man credit, he was sharp as a three-penny nail. And she was glad he would be her defense attorney if things didn't go their way.

Chase looked at his watch as if it helped him calculate. "Our appointment with you was at two-thirty so I'd guess the shots were fired between two and two fifteen."

Bradley spoke with satisfaction. "I don't even know if Sally owns a gun but I'm glad questioning her won't be necessary."

"I'm sorry I had to ask," Laura apologized without responding to Bradley's statement. She still intended to speak with Sally. Chase gave her a long look of understanding, knowing that they had to question every woman even remotely involved since Lance suspected Brent's murderer might have been female. Besides, maybe she'd seen something that would prove useful.

"And while I was in the courthouse, speaking to the sheriff today about you, Judge Perkins could have overheard," Bradley said.

Laura threw her hands into the air in disgust. "Just great. The judge at my trial is one of our suspects."

"Somehow I can't picture Perkins trying to ambush you with a rifle, either. And besides, what motive could he have had to kill Brent?"

"We need to find out," Chase muttered.

"I'd advise you to put the judge last on your list. He's not going to appreciate that you suspect him of murder, and we need his goodwill during the trial." Bradley shifted in his chair. "You might also want to check Lance's whereabouts at three o'clock. Are there any bullets in your vehicle?''

"Probably." Chase nodded. "One of them's embedded in the seat's back.''

"Don't touch it," Bradley instructed. "We'll have the sheriff dig it out. Maybe we can at least identify what type of rifle fired it.''

Laura leaned forward, resting her elbows on her knees. "Will that help?''

Bradley shrugged. "We can't afford to overlook anything. Because we still don't have a shred of hard evidence that anyone killed Brent except for your fingerprints on the pitchfork or who killed Tyler except hair that looks like it could be yours that was found at his murder scene.''

Laura bit her bottom lip. "But Lance's testimony—''

"You claim you went out the barn's front door. Can you prove it?''

Laura sighed with frustration. Without looking at Chase she knew he felt just as stymied as she did. They might be gathering clues but all they had were conjectures, suspicions, a whole bunch of nothing.

Chase stood and paced, his voice forceful. "We can prove someone shot at my truck.''

The dog opened one sleepy eye, decided Chase wasn't a threat despite the growl in his tone, and went back to sleep. Bradley upended his glass and set it down with care. "The sheriff may not believe your story.''

Chase pivoted on his heel and drilled Bradley with a stare. "Why not?''

"He's not inclined to change his mind after he thinks he's already caught the killer. No one saw the

shooter, not even you two. You have no one to corroborate your story.''

"I have bullet holes in my truck!''

"Which you could have shot yourself to take suspicion off Laura.''

She didn't like the way Bradley had destroyed
their hopes of proving her innocence. "Whose side
are you on?''

"Please,'' Bradley held up his hand, "I have to
think like a prosecutor to counter his arguments.''

"So what are we going to do?'' Laura asked, ticking off points on her fingers. "Our questions are
making the killer nervous. That's why he shot at me.
To shut me up before we find him—or her.'' And
while she was a target, she was endangering the
lives of whoever was near her. Chase could have
died tonight because he was with her, trying to help
her and at the thought, her stomach clenched into a
roiling cauldron of acid.

"Your theory is possible,'' Bradley admitted.
"But I need proof to present in court. Planting
doubts in the jury's minds isn't good enough.''

"What about reasonable doubt?'' Chase asked.

Bradley shook his head. "Against hard evidence?''

"What do you suggest?'' Laura asked, her voice
rising with anxiety despite her efforts to remain calm.

Chase took her hand and gently pulled her to her
feet. "We keep digging.''

And hoped no one put her in jail or killed her
before they solved the murder.

FRANCESCA MARTIN, THE sheriff's dispatcher, lived
alone in one of the new condos that was short on

space but long on a spectacular view of the mountains. She didn't seem surprised to see them show up at her doorstep unannounced the next evening but didn't invite them inside either, instead suggesting they drive to a local bar.

Chase wondered if the plain female was hiding someone behind her front door, was embarrassed over a messy place, wanted a free dinner or just wanted to go out. She seemed lonely and kept twirling her hair around her finger, either a nervous gesture or a practiced one that drew attention to her best feature: her blond hair. Vulnerable with that desperate look in her eyes that single women sometimes have when they hear their biological clocks ticking, Francesca didn't strike him as a killer, but maybe she could tell them something useful.

The dispatcher suggested a local cop hangout that boasted a tinny-sounding jukebox, two pool tables and the latest video games. A waitress took their order, fluttering her eyelashes at Chase. He handed back the menu, ignoring the waitress's attention. Everyone in town knew the Sutton boys, and he'd heard single women gossiped endlessly about their chances of catching one. Many were attracted to the Suttons' wealth and power. Chase was too solid and serious to enjoy casual flirtations. He didn't like games, said what he meant, and he flat out had no interest in the cocktail waitress who finally got the message and brought back their drinks.

After downing half a shot of whiskey in one long swallow, Francesca set down her glass and leaned across the table toward Laura and Chase. "What can I tell you?"

Chase fiddled with his beer, knowing he had to be careful not to antagonize the sheriff's dispatcher. He sensed the wrong question would send Francesca fleeing to her cop buddies for help. "I understand your mother works for my father."

"So?"

Beneath the table, Laura squeezed his hand tight, signaling him to back off. She spoke softly, more gently than he would have. "Please, I need your help. We're looking for anyone who might have seen a woman in the barn the night of Brent's murder."

"I finished my chores early and I was studying that night." Francesca held up her hand before Laura could ask another question. "And no, I don't have an alibi, but I also had no reason to kill him. He never came on to me, at least not after…"

"Not after what?" Laura asked.

Francesca licked her lips, finished her whiskey and Chase signaled the waitress for another. As much as Chase wanted to demand answers from the woman, he had to admit, Laura's pleading tone and begging eyes were more sympathetic.

Francesca lit a cigarette and remained silent until her drink arrived. This time she sipped more slowly and Chase's first impression of her as a possible alcoholic changed. She'd needed the drink to fortify her courage, but she still seemed frightened.

"What did you mean, Brent never came on to you?" Laura asked.

Smart woman. There were more ways to ask questions than head-on and Laura had the sense to try another tactic. Chase couldn't help but admire her clear thinking after all she'd been through.

Francesca blew out a ring of smoke. "Brent's proclivities were the reason I'm an expert shot." The dispatcher sent them a sardonic grin. "My mother insisted that Lance teach me how to shoot and demanded that I carry the weapon with me at all times."

"Because of my brother?" Chase asked.

"You sound so surprised." Francesca played with her wet napkin, nervous fingers shredding the edges. "Oh, I guess Brent was okay when he was sober—but when he drank, which was all too often…he turned…nasty. Violent."

Laura ignored her drink. "He ever turn on you?"

"Only once. I pulled my gun…didn't have to shoot him. But I would have if it had been necessary." She sounded unconvincing instead of tough and Chase wondered if she really could have pulled the trigger. "But he never bothered me again," she stated, a flat look dulling her eyes.

While the dispatcher admitted to knowing how to shoot and could have fired the shots from the mountain, if she was a murderer, then why hadn't she shot Brent, not stabbed him with a pitchfork? Still it was best to be sure.

"Can you tell me your whereabouts between two and three yesterday?" Chase asked.

"A.m. or p.m.?"

"Afternoon."

Francesca stubbed out her cigarette in an overflowing ashtray. "One of these days I'm going to quit." Chase suspected she was stalling, deciding whether or not to answer his question. "I was making love with a married cop. I hope you don't need his name because I won't tell you."

An alibi they couldn't check. Still the sadness in her eyes convinced Chase the woman was hiding something.

"Do you know any women who might have held a grudge against Brent?" Laura asked.

Francesca sighed and lit another cigarette. "Sally Walker. I think she's Mark Bradley's secretary now. She hated him, but I don't know why."

Damn! Sally Walker had black hair, not blond. Still, maybe she could help them. But when Chase called her home, her roommate told them Sally was an avid camper and had taken off for the weekend. They'd have to wait until Monday to ask their questions.

"WHERE'RE WE HEADED?" Laura asked Chase, settling Keith before her in the saddle.

But the toddler wriggled and twisted, holding his arms out to his father. "Daddy. Up, Daddy."

Chase guided his horse beside her until their knees touched. "I'll take him."

"You sure you don't mind? He's a handful."

"Like his mother." Chase chuckled as heat filled her cheeks at his innuendo.

Laura handed Chase their son and wished she could spend more time riding. As much as she'd enjoyed New Orleans, city life hadn't agreed with her. Neither had being cooped up in an office doing title work. She'd much rather gallop across the open spaces than research titles and pore through plat books. The Embry ranch was home. This land was her future. Keith's future.

Her son smiled happily as he picked up the end of the reins and chewed. Gently, Chase took the leather from his mouth and distracted him by pointing out a calf. "Baby cow."

Chase was patient with Keith and it made her heart ache to see them riding together, the man so straight and tall, the child bouncing around the saddle and giggling happily. They had an entire day to spend together as a family and she wanted to make the most of it.

"Your father wants me to check on some fence line. We've lost a few cows. They may have wandered over onto the Senator's land...."

"But you don't think so?"

"The Senator claims he's missing cattle, too."

In summertime, the ranchers let the cows wander into the foothills where grass was plentiful. If the herds mixed, the cowboys could discern the owners from their brands. But first they had to find them. The cows often bunched around the water, refusing to leave one area and overgrazing until there was no grass left, only dirt and mud. "Maybe they're at the river."

"Let's hope so."

At the finality in Chase's tone, she knew he wanted her to stop speculating. She supposed he needed a break from their troubles as much as she did, maybe more so. Relations between him and his family had to be strained, but to Chase's credit, he never mentioned the awkward position that being with her put him in. He never complained, either.

Laura gathered her courage. "There's something I've been wanting to talk to you about." When he remained silent, she let out a sigh, knowing he wouldn't like this subject either, but she needed him to listen. "Being around me is dangerous to your health. I don't think we should go into town together anymore.''

"I'm not leaving you unprotected.'' There was no compromise in his hard tone.

"I appreciate the sentiment and your company— more than you can know.''

"Good.'' He settled his hat lower on his head and turned silent on her as if he considered the conversation over.

"But we have to think of Keith.''

"Keith needs a mother. I may be his favorite playmate right now, but he never lets *you* out of his sight. And when he gets hurt, it's you he turns to for comfort.''

She was amazed that he'd noticed and then didn't know why that was so. Chase was a keen judge of character. He could read animals and people's hearts as easily as the Senator read his constituents' minds—which made arguing with Chase all the more difficult.

"I don't want him to lose *both* of us. And—''

"I won't let that happen.''

"Chase, be reasonable. If we're together and someone comes after me, we could both be killed.''

Chase scratched his chin. "Maybe we haven't been looking at this right. Don't you find it odd that someone is going to all this trouble to frame you for murder and then trying to kill you?''

"Maybe he's afraid I know something that could point the finger at the real murderer. So they try to kill me to shut me up. If they succeed, all the loose strings are tied up. With me dead, the murders may never be solved.''

"We'll figure out the mystery before that happens.'' His cocksure attitude irritated her, especially since she didn't think they were any closer to figuring out who the murderer was.

Laura let out a long sigh. Chase could be twice as stubborn as a jackass.

They rode over a rise and she stopped her mount to take in the magnificent view. But her mind wouldn't stay focused on the multitude of greens, the richness of the land. "I can't figure it out. Lance thinks he saw a woman come out of the barn after Brent's death. And long blond hair was found at Tyler's. Sally has dark hair and Francesca has an alibi. We have no suspects.''

"Someone is lying, maybe Lance. Or Sally could have planted hair at the scene and Francesca's alibi might not hold up. We just have to scratch up enough facts until we figure out the truth. The Senator is discretely questioning Francesca's lover to see if he'll corroborate her alibi.''

"How does the Senator know who her lover is? She wouldn't tell us.''

"Sometimes it's best not to question his sources.''

Laura cocked an eyebrow.

Chase sighed. "Dad might have a friend at the phone company. And Cam is doing background checks on Lance and Judge Perkins.''

"Please, thank them for me." Was that Chase's secret? That his family was trying to help them? Or was his family trying to eliminate any possibility of other people's guilt so the prosecution would have a stronger case against her?

"We have company." Chase pointed to a downed fence between the Embry and Sutton ranches and several riders herding cattle. He urged his mount forward down the gentle slope, then gradually settled his horse into a canter as the rocky hillside gave way to flat pasture land.

Keith whooped with glee and Laura was glad to see Chase's arm firmly wrapped around his waist, holding him safe. She supposed she should have been nervous, but her earliest memories were of the wind flying through her hair, her father holding her much the way Chase held Keith and tears brimmed in her eyes. She wanted to make more babies with Chase. She wanted to watch them grow up on Embry land and she wanted to spoil her grandchildren the way her mother did Keith.

Two of the hands had ridden off long before they arrived and Laura hung back as she watched Chase greet the Senator, Cam and Rafe, but she stayed close enough to see the Senator's gaze hungrily stare at his grandson. He shook Chase's hand with a formality that surprised her, then he shook the toddler's hand, too.

Keith must have liked what he saw because he held out his arms to the Senator. "Up."

Her stomach knotted at the tenderness in the Senator's eyes as without hesitation he took the baby onto his horse. There could be no doubting how much the Senator wanted to claim his grandson. He couldn't take his eyes off Keith, even examining his fingers and bare toes.

"Hey! Share." Cam rode up, tapped the Senator on the shoulder and held out his arms. "I want to meet my nephew."

While the Senator was clearly reluctant to let go, Keith thought he'd just found a new game. He eagerly went to Cam who promptly tossed the baby a few inches into the air and caught him.

"Careful." The words popped out of Chase's mouth before she could say them.

She bit back a warning, unwilling to spoil this first meeting between her son and Chase's family. Laura knew about Cam's thriving medical practice in Boston, his wealthy wife and their twins. She reminded herself the man was a father, a doctor, and unlikely to hurt her child even accidentally. Besides, she couldn't deny him the pure pleasure in making the baby giggle until his dimples showed.

Keith chuckled with glee. "More. More. More," he demanded. "Go high."

Surrounded by four big Sutton men, all dark-haired and gray eyed, Laura felt in awe that her son was not the least bit intimidated. Instead he seemed one of them, albeit a miniature version. But he exhibited the same fearlessness, a reckless gleam in his six-toothed smile, a happy disregard for danger. She envisioned him thriving on this great piece of open land with his father and grandfather and uncles to guide him. The Sutton family was strong, held together by the land, loyalty and love, their roots spread as wide as the vast acreage.

She need have no fears for her son's future without her. And yet she ached to be a part of his life and watch him mature. Some anxiety must have shown on her face because Cam thought to reassure her. The largest of the brothers, he was a thick mountain of muscle and possessed the gentlest of smiles.

"Don't worry." Cam's big hands closed around

Keith's waist and tossed him higher. "I've had plenty of practice with my two hellions."

Rafe, tall and whipcord lean, tilted back his hat, rakish mischief gleaming in his dark eyes. "And how many times did you drop them?"

"As I recall," Chase butted into the teasing, "the only one Cam ever dropped…was you. Knocked you out cold."

"He was aiming to lasso you," Rafe muttered.

Chase grinned. "And I had the good sense to duck the rope."

From their jesting tones, Laura knew the injury hadn't been serious and the brothers had forgiven one another long ago. Still, Cam was slow to anger. If he had a temper, he hid it well. To swing a lasso at Chase, he must have been furious.

"What did you do to make Cam angry?" she asked Chase, curious and determined not to let the men keep her an outsider in the conversation.

Chase tried and failed to look innocent. "I only saddled his bull."

"My breeding bull," Cam clarified. "The one I'd raised from a calf for 4-H. The animal trusted people until my fool brothers tried to ride him."

"Rafe dared me," Chase muttered as if that were a good excuse.

Rafe rolled his eyes.

"Actually, you did me a favor," Cam said as he handed the baby back to the Senator.

"I did?" Chase asked.

"Well, Rafe did. When I saw I'd roped and knocked Rafe on his sorry ass and couldn't wake him up, I decided to become a doctor."

"And now you have a great career, thanks to

me.'' Rafe bowed in the saddle. ''Maybe you should pay me a commission for helping start you out.''

''Listen, buzzard bait,'' Cam said using his pet name for Rafe. He swung off his horse and started to mend broken barbed wire. ''I'm well aware that after you recovered, you rode that bull to a standstill.''

Rafe whistled jauntily. ''My way of getting back at you, beef cake.''

Laura restrained her smile at the insultingly affectionate nicknames.

''Boys, we've got work to do.'' The Senator kept Keith in his saddle. ''Rafe, help your brother with the fence. We don't need to open the door for the rustlers.''

Chase didn't dismount to help as Laura expected. Instead he turned to his father. ''Any news?''

The Senator fingered his cigar, looked at the baby and left the unlit cigar in his pocket. ''Cam's investigation of Lance turned up nothing. As far as we can tell, the mechanic is a good worker and had no grudge against Brent.''

''And Judge Perkins?'' Laura asked.

''He's honest.''

Chase frowned. ''As long as you're doing background investigations, see what you can turn up on Sally Walker, Bradley's secretary.''

The Senator cocked his head, thinking out loud. ''She worked in the barn, mucking out stalls, back then. And our female workers always wear gloves so that would account for a lack of prints on the weapon—but she's a brunette.''

''Hair could have been planted or she could have worn a wig,'' Laura suggested. ''Francesca told us

Sally had an intense dislike of Brent. Would any of you know why?''

The men shook their heads. The Senator took a handful of keys out of his pocket and handed them to Keith who promptly tried to stuff them in his mouth.

''I did find one very interesting fact about the lady dispatcher.''

''She doesn't have a lover?'' Chase guessed.

''We found him, all right. But he claims the lady left him by noon.''

''She lied to us, then,'' Laura said.

''She might just have been alone and unable to account for her time,'' the Senator suggested.

Chase scowled. ''Or she might have been shooting at my truck as we drove into town.''

At Chase's fierce scowl, Laura took his hand. ''We need to speak to her again.''

''Yeah, but first thing Monday morning, I want to talk to the suspiciously missing Sally Walker.''

The ride back to the Embry ranch was uneventful. Keith slept in his father's arms and after they arrived, Chase dismounted and carried him into the house.

Laura took both horses into the barn. Since they'd walked the last mile, the horses were already cooled down. She led them to water, removed their saddles, then eased her mount into her stall. Her well-trained horse willingly cooperated, but Chase's gelding snorted and pawed, the high-strung animal probably nervous around a new handler.

''Come on, sweetie,'' Laura crooned, taking the reins and leading him into the stall.

The whisper of a rattle had the horse rearing onto

his hind legs, yanking the reins from Laura's hands. Dodging the flailing horse's hooves, she slipped to the animal's side. And again heard a deadly rattle.

Head raised and angry, a snake lay coiled less than a foot from where Laura stood.

Chapter Nine

Chase had just handed Keith over to Anna Embry for a bath when a sharp scream, Laura's scream, sent him vaulting down the hallway and down the porch steps. Adrenaline sped his footsteps as he sprinted across the front yard and down the path to the Embry barn.

He shouldn't have left Laura alone for a second and damned himself for his assumption that she would be safe on home ground. Heart pumping, he careened around the barn's corner, skidding on loose dirt and hay, cursing the cowboy boots that were not meant for running.

He raced into the barn, followed the screams of his unruly gelding whinnying hair-raising snorts and pounding the wooden rails of the stall with his hooves. His horse reared and he prayed that Laura had avoided the deadly hooves.

Laura!

Chase rounded the stall, frantic for a sight of her. When he spied her, lying so still on her side, her back to the far wall, his heart danced into his throat.

"Don't come in here," she screamed at him.

Standing helpless and immobile while his woman was stomped to death wasn't an option.

Unsaddled, reins trailing the ground, the gelding bucked and kicked, his front hooves missing Laura's head by inches. Unsure what had set the horse off, Chase moved expertly to the animal's side, grabbed the loose reins and attempted to pull the berserk gelding away from her.

"Get back! There's a snake."

Chase looked down, shuddered at the sight of a coiled snake, its tail rattling, readying to strike Laura's face. Without hesitation, he released the horse, yanked the snake by the tail and bashed the rattler's head against the concrete water trough in one frantic move.

His horse seemed to understand the snake was no longer a threat and stopped bucking almost immediately. Shivering and shuddering to a standstill, he pawed his front hooves nervously through the hay as if wary that another snake might have invaded his stall.

Chase knelt by Laura. "Were you bit?"

"Your horse saved me."

He ran his hands over her arms and legs, searching for broken bones. "Are you hurt?"

Her face was pale, her eyes looking too big, her pupils dilated. Blood trickling from a small cut at her forehead, she winced and slowly regained her feet, leaning into him. "Just a few bruises."

He slung his arm around her waist and helped her from the stall. She looked back over her shoulder. "Your horse still has the bridle—"

"It's you I'm worried about, but I'll send one of the hands to take care of him."

''He saved my life.''

She trembled against his arm and he damned himself for leaving her alone. ''Are you sure you weren't bitten?''

''Would you like to check me for bite marks?'' she teased weakly.

''How can you make jokes?'' he marveled at her strength, then as she sagged against him, he realized she was operating on automatic and more shaken than she'd admitted. ''Here, let me help you to the house.''

Anna opened the Embry front door, and when she saw Laura leaning heavily on him, her face tightened in alarm. ''What happened?''

''I'm fine, Mom, just a little shaky. Please make sure Keith is okay and I'll be inside in a minute.''

Anna ducked back inside, leaving them alone on the porch except for the chirps of crickets and an early night owl hooting at the newly risen crescent moon. Chase held Laura back for a moment, then swung her into his arms. She placed her cheek against his chest, her hands around his neck and scooped her into his arms. She had a smudge of dirt on her cheek, and her lips were much too pale and he'd never thought she looked so beautiful. She was alive and he wanted her. Not just in a sexual away. But he wanted her in the way a man needs to draw his next breath, takes it, then needs another to go on. He would never have enough of her. She was his soul mate, his love and he wanted her by his side forever.

The strength of his feelings staggered him. She was his family, the mother of his son, his life mate and irreplaceable. If he lost her, he might not recover. His throat tightened and he swallowed the lump in his throat, the depth of his emotions silencing him.

He sat on the front stoop and kept her on his lap, cuddling her, enjoying the feel of her husky breath against his neck, her quivering skin on his cheek, her lips blue as he dipped his head and took her mouth to warm her in the way he knew best.

She tasted sweet and smooth. Just a taste and his breath grew ragged. "I could have lost you."

"I'm okay." She pulled back and gazed into his eyes, her expression a mixture of passion and confusion. "Do you think the snake slithered into that stall all by himself?"

The implication of her question floored him. He'd been too busy worrying over her to consider the ramifications of the incident, but once she forced the issue, he shook his head. "Snakes like the chicken coop better."

"So someone put it there."

"I should have been with you. I'm sorry. I'll do better in the—"

"The snake was in *your* horse's stall."

He'd been so concerned about her, he hadn't fully thought through the incident. His head was dazed with holding her, his nostrils enthralled with her scent that made him dizzy with desire.

Think with your brains. "What are you saying?"

"If the snake was deliberately put in *your* horse's stall, then someone wanted *you* dead."

"Me?" He caressed a tendril of hair from her eyes. "Why would anyone be after me?"

"Because you're protecting me," she suggested. "Or maybe I've never been the target."

"What! We're investigating a murder where you are the prime suspect. If you died, we could never prove your innocence and the real killer would go free. Therefore the killer is after you. But he can't have you—not when I want you so much."

She gripped him tight. "Suppose we've been making incorrect assumptions?"

"Like what?"

"Someone killed Brent—who was the eldest Sutton son. Then they killed Tyler, the next eldest. Suppose they're after you—the next in line to inherit the Sutton ranch?"

Stunned by her theory, he couldn't help seeing the logic in her thinking but he wasn't sure he agreed. "Every attack has been—"

"—when we were together. Maybe the shooter was trying to kill you. The snake was in your horse's stall. Bullets were aimed at your truck and concentrated on the driver's side."

"The driver's side of the truck was closer to the shooter. And maybe the snake crawled in there by himself."

"You didn't think so a few minutes ago," she pointed out. "Did you, Brent and Tyler ever date the same girl?"

He followed her thinking but doubted the possibility. "I can't know for sure, but I doubt it. Brent liked easy women and Tyler was attracted to arty types."

"And you? What type do you like?" she asked, her tone gaining a husky purr.

He grinned down at her, unable to contain a teasing smile. "I prefer the type that falls into my lap."

DESPITE LAURA'S NEW theory, she and Chase were both anxious to speak with Sally Walker on Monday morning. They caught up with Bradley's busy secretary at the doughnut shop where she'd stopped for a midmorning snack.

The dark-haired Sally Walker spotted them as they entered the busy establishment and waved them over with a friendly grin. "Bradley said you wanted to talk with me."

Chase and Laura slipped into seats across the table from her, the scent of hot cinnamon, apples and powdered sugar filling their noses. Laura's mouth watered but she really ached for coffee and a caffeine pick-me-up.

While Laura wished Bradley hadn't warned his secretary, she wasn't surprised the sharp attorney had realized Laura still intended to question the woman—even after he'd given her an alibi.

Chase signaled a waitress for coffee. "We were wondering if you could help us with a few loose ends."

Sally leaned forward and bit into a sugar doughnut. "How can I help?"

"What time did you close the office on Thursday?" Laura asked, sure she would confirm Bradley's statement.

"Let's see." Sally reached into her purse and took out an electronic daytimer. "Mark, I mean Mr. Bradley," she blushed, "was in court until three. I had errands to run and closed the office early."

Chase frowned. "Bradley said you closed at five."

"I usually do. But my mother was sick and I had

to run errands for her. I never told Bradley I closed early.''

Laura recalled the secretary reading a book when they first entered the office. Now she admitted to closing early without notifying her boss—but that made her a poor employee, not a killer. Sally must have read the look on her face.

''Mark won't mind. I'm going to quit soon. It's still a secret but I guess I can tell you.'' She leaned forward and whispered excitedly, a happy grin on her face. ''We're going to marry as soon as your trial is over.''

A flutter of anxiety shook Laura. Suppose Sally had killed Brent then confessed to Bradley? Had the attorney counseled his lover to keep quiet? After Laura returned to Colorado had they tried to pin the second murder on her? And how convenient that Judge Stewart, Bradley's old law partner had posted her bail—letting her free so she could appear guilty.

Laura took a deep breath, knowing she was over-reacting, knowing she was seeing conspiracies everywhere. Especially since Bradley and Sally hadn't even bothered to get their stories and alibis straight. Especially since yesterday Laura had believed the killer was after Chase and not her. Sally looked so eager to marry, innocent and joyful and in love. And the thought of Highview's most prominent attorney teaming up with a federal judge to commit murder seemed ludicrous.

''What errands did you run for your mother?'' Chase asked Sally.

''The usual. Dry cleaning, filling prescriptions, grocery shopping? Why?''

Luckily Highview only had two dry cleaning establishments, one grocery store and one pharmacy. Sally's story could easily be checked without asking her for specifics.

"We just stopped by the office that day and were surprised to find it closed," Chase lied, obviously unwilling to reveal to Sally that she was on their list of suspects. "The reason we wanted to talk to you was because you worked at the ranch during the time Brent was murdered. We were hoping you might have seen something or know something to help us."

Sally's brows drew together in a frown. "Like what?"

"Lance told us he saw a woman leave the barn after Brent's death. Do you have any idea who she could have been?"

Sally shrugged. "Brent liked lots of girls but he preferred blondes. He had several girlfriends, no one serious that I knew about. Or Lance could have seen one of the exercise girls or one of the stall muckers leaving the barn. Have you checked the employment records?"

"We'll question everyone," Laura told her. "Apparently, Brent wasn't...well liked."

Sally tapped her nails on the table, clearly unwilling to respond to Laura's statement voluntarily. She evaded Chase's eyes, staring down into her coffee dregs. "I was in the barn the night of Brent's murder but I left before dark. I heard him mention he had plans," she shivered and raised her head, staring out the window. "I'm sorry that your brother died, but I can't help remembering his tone of voice, the way he bragged about his plans. He'd been drinking all day. He sounded...ugly."

"He was meeting a woman?" Chase asked.

"I assumed so."

"But you don't know who?"

Sally looked at Laura as if embarrassed, then looked away. "He said a blond-haired bitch who needed a lesson. I didn't think he meant anything by it. I assumed it was just the liquor talking."

"Did you tell the sheriff any of this?" Chase asked.

"No."

Laura's voice rose in indignation. "Why not?"

"Nobody asked me." Sally shrugged. "And besides, why speak ill of the dead? After all, I worked for the Suttons. I thought I was being loyal to keep my mouth shut."

"How well did you know Francesca Martin?" Laura asked, realizing they still needed more facts to pursue their investigation.

"Her mother was the Senator's cook. They boarded a horse in the barn for free and Francesca often came to visit her mom and ride. She didn't talk to the likes of the stable hands, though."

"Was she around my brother much?"

"She was blond, wasn't she? As I said, Brent had a thing for blondes. I believe he may have taken her for a ride a time or two."

Sally didn't specify what kind of ride, but from her tone she'd left little to the imagination. Strange that Francesca hadn't admitted any relationship with Brent, instead implying that Sally Walker had hated the Sutton heir. But Sally spoke about Brent matter-of-factly, as if his behavior hadn't mattered to her at all. So either Sally was covering up her true feelings, Francesca was lying or Sally's hatred for Brent had dulled over time.

"Someone told us that you hated Brent Sutton," Laura stated baldly, hoping to elicit a reaction.

"He wasn't my favorite person but as I said before there's no point in speaking badly of those who have passed on." Sally picked up a box of doughnuts and stood. "If there's nothing else, I'd better head back to the office."

After the secretary left, Laura looked at Chase. "What do you think?"

"That I want to talk with Francesca again. She lied about her alibi. She hid her relationship with my brother and she implied Sally hated Brent. Either Sally is a very good actress or Francesca was spinning us a story. Either way, I want to know why."

FRANCESCA WOULDN'T BE available to talk with them until her lunch break so they had several hours of free time to spend in Highview. With tourist season in full swing, the traffic was thicker than normal, the heat oppressive. An invasion of outsiders had turned the sleepy town into a bustling community intent on siphoning off tourist dollars.

As they left the doughnut shop, Laura took Chase's hand and steered him down the street. He peered at her beneath the brim of his hat, then leaned forward to wipe a bit of powered sugar off her chin. "Where're you taking me?"

"Let's do some research at the library," she suggested, conspiracy theories pumping through her head, until Chase brought his sugary finger to her mouth. She shook her head. "No thanks."

With a nonchalant shrug, he licked the sugar off

his own finger and she couldn't help wishing those lips were back on hers. Chase Sutton was her dream man and not just because she found his dark eyes fascinating, his smile enchanting. She liked the way he focused on her, making her feel as if she were the most important person in the world to him. She liked a man with the confidence to know what he wanted, the ability to pursue his goals and the determination to succeed. His convictions boosted hers, making her feel both more feminine and more capable.

The library's interior, brighter and smaller than she remembered, was a cool welcome after the early-morning heat. The microfiche files were just where she remembered them.

They walked past a row of study cubicles and Chase pulled her inside one and shut the door behind him. She looked up at his mischievous grin, at his eyes that caressed her and her pulse sped up a notch. She realized the heat inside her had nothing to do with summer weather. ''Yes?''

He took her into his arms for a hug. ''I've been wanting to do this all morning.''

''Is that so?'' She tilted her head back and leaned into his chest, pleased by the muscled hardness that complimented her softness.

''Do that again,'' he murmured.

''What?''

''Rub up against me like a starved cat.''

Biting back a grin of pleasure that he liked her aggressiveness, she slid sinuously against him. When his mouth came down on hers, she kissed him back, wishing they didn't have to steal moments of love between their murder investigation. If only they had more time. But she was grateful for what they had, glad she was out on bail.

Her lips swelled beneath Chase's attentions and she had to make herself pull back. Both of them had difficulty controlling their breathing and he was looking at her as if he wanted to take off her clothes and have her for a snack on the minidesk. The way he had her heart humming, she wouldn't mind— except one of them had to be an adult.

She chewed her bottom lip, fighting the surge of heat in her. "These cubicles don't have locks."

"I just wanted a taste of you." He removed his hat and threaded his hand through his hair, his voice husky. "But now I'm starving for more."

She eyed the bulge in his jeans. "I've already been arrested for murder. I'd hate to add indecent exposure to my list of crimes."

At her words, his eyes widened in surprise, fired with passion. "I didn't mean to—"

"Shh!" She raised a finger to his lips. "Kiss me."

She'd unleashed madness. He backed her against the desk, and she was melting, swimming in currents of hot and cold, fire and ice. The world shrank to this tiny cubicle and his lips.

The scent of coffee and doughnuts and Chase swirled around her in a sensual haze. She had to bite her lip from releasing a moan. His hands on her back, his lips on hers, felt so good. Amazed at the sizzling storm of sensuality that electrified her body, she tried to gather her frothing thoughts, but they were carried away in swirling eddies of sensation.

She'd never been aware of Chase like this, sensing his very heat, anticipating his every breath. Florescent lighting caught his dark hair in a metallic glow, his tawny skin seemed so alive, his face wore the most beautiful predatory expression she'd ever seen. His eyes glinted with an intimacy and intensity that had her wanting more.

His mouth was hard, proud and hungry. Mostly hungry.

Frantic with need, barely thinking on a coherent level, she forgot where she was and closed her eyes, barely able to bear the exquisite intimacy of his kiss. She only knew feeling, sensation and the hunger this man could feed.

With a groan, Chase pulled back and it took moments, maybe minutes before she could begin to gather her thoughts. That she had lost herself so completely in such a public place astounded and worried her.

She couldn't imagine what Chase must think. And yet, she wouldn't have taken back that searing kiss if she could have. With a murder trial and a conviction hanging over her head like a guillotine blade about to drop, she felt little guilt over shared pleasure with Chase. For a moment, their lips and hearts and desires fused, and they'd become as one.

Chapter Ten

Eventually Laura and Chase got around to researching old newspaper files in the library. The kiss in the cubicle had been amazing; her nerve endings were still tingling from Chase's tenderness, but there would be few more moments like those if she didn't keep her mind focused on finding who had set her up. That person had robbed almost two years from Chase and Keith, preventing father and son from knowing one another. She couldn't allow more time to be stolen from those she loved.

And she loved Chase Sutton with all her heart. Yet she wasn't ready to tell him. What would be the point when she might be spending the rest of her life behind bars? She wouldn't do that to him, wouldn't tell him of her love and burden him with hope for a future that might never be.

Instead, she concentrated on the task of reading hundreds of articles on the Sutton family, searching for an enemy, something or someone that could account for a killer going after the Sutton boys. Unfortunately the Senator's political agenda created too many foes to count. Every time he ran for election, every time he voted on legislation, someone or some group held an opposing view. And then she ran across the endless land and water and grazing disputes that seemed a perpetual problem in cow country. Feuds over property lines could span generations. Without more to go on, Laura and Chase had been forced to temporarily give up.

Laura hoped Francesca Martin would be more helpful the second time around and tensed as she and Chase entered the sheriff's office. While the weak air-conditioning and lazy whizzing fan cooled her, Laura barely noticed. She was too pumped for a confrontation. She wanted to know why Francesca had lied to them and she wouldn't be satisfied until she had her answers.

Beside her, Chase's eyes had a hard edge to them. His neck corded and his eyes glinted like shiny steel pools. A feral quality enhanced his steps as if he were a hunter after prey. One glance at his dark determination and Laura was very glad he was on her side.

She looked for the sheriff's dispatcher. Francesca should be on her way to lunch any time now, and Laura hoped the element of surprise would work to their advantage. Francesca would be surprised they knew of her lies, and Laura prayed if they pushed hard enough, the woman would make a mistake, perhaps reveal a clue to the killer's identity.

The sheriff looked up as they entered, giving a polite nod to Chase, but the sarcasm in his voice was unmistakable. "Good afternoon, folks. Anyone else shot at you lately?"

Chase smiled grimly. "Did the bullets you dug out of my truck tell you anything?" Chase deftly put the sheriff in his place, clearly not caring who heard.

From her dispatcher's station behind a waist-high counter, Francesca fielded a radio call from a squad car but was clearly enjoying the sight of her boss turning crimson with anger.

The sheriff cleared his throat and hitched up his pants. "There are no identifying marks on those bullets after they went through metal. And the bullets could have been fired from one of a hundred similar rifles in this county—including yours. Those bullets were a waste of the lab's time. My theory is that you shot those—"

"We don't care to hear *your* theory, Sheriff," Chase cut in. "We want results."

Laura tried to hide her disappointment at the inconclusive forensic tests. She'd been hoping that the sheriff would believe their story and start investigating the possibility that someone besides her had committed a crime.

"On the other hand," the sheriff continued with a satisfied grunt, "I'm expecting a DNA analysis of the hair I found to turn up a match with Ms. Embry—"

"Even if it's a match," Chase drawled, his eyes the color of winter, "that doesn't prove she killed anyone."

Quietly and with a minimum of fuss, Francesca had gathered her purse and started to sidle out the door. Laura tugged on Chase's elbow and followed the dispatcher without another word to the obstinate sheriff. If he wouldn't listen to reason, they'd have to solve the puzzle themselves, and Laura wasn't about to let their suspect evade the interrogation she had planned.

When Francesca noticed them following her, alarm flared in her eyes. Laura thought she might run and was surprised when the woman halted without warning on the busy sidewalk, spun around, her blond hair flying, and glared at them. "I've answered all the questions I'm going to."

"Fine," Chase agreed, but his lips grimaced with anger and stubbornness. "We'll have Bradley deposition you, and you can explain to the court why you lied about where you were the day someone fired shots at us."

At his bald accusation, Francesca paled. She swung her head from side to side, clearly uncomfortable in the spotlight of the crowd gawking on the sidewalk around them. "I've only an hour for my lunch. I don't have to spend it talking to you." She scowled at Laura. "I'm sure you didn't mean to kill Brent. It was an accident, wasn't it? Why don't you just tell these good citizens why you stabbed your lover's brother in the throat?"

"In the throat?" Laura's heart battered her ribs, and she grabbed Francesca's wrist, afraid the woman might try to run. "How do you know Brent was stabbed in the throat?"

Francesca blanched another shade whiter. "It must have been in the newspaper."

"It wasn't," said someone in the crowd.

The townsfolk pressed closer, their demeanor hostile, and Laura hoped it would rattle Francesca.

"So how do you know?" Chase moved in, his face predatory and arrogant, as if warning Francesca not to try another lie.

"I m-must have seen the autopsy r-report," Francesca stammered, but her chin remained high, her shoulders squared to do battle.

"The sheriff keeps them locked up tight," Laura persisted, knowing she had to attack the woman, sensing a weakness that hadn't been there the last time they'd spoken. She had the feeling that Francesca knew more, much more than she'd told them. Her frightened face, her lies, the stammer, all added up to a guilty conscience.

Although every nerve was thrumming to prove her own innocence, Laura needed proof—and she was not about to let this woman keep it from her. If she knew something crucial, Laura would keep battering her with questions until her secret spilled free.

"Maybe I heard the uniforms talking about Brent's death," Francesca said, but her tone was unconvincing. "It's been so long, I'm not sure."

"You saw the body that night, didn't you?" Chase kept his voice soft but Laura never doubted the threat in it. "You saw the stab wounds in the throat. Did you kill him?"

"Of course not!" Francesca objected, her eyes wide, her voice trembling.

At the commotion on the sidewalk, the sheriff had made his way outside, the skinny man slipping through the crowd to Francesca's side. "Let's go back to my office where we can talk." He raised his arms and shooed people along. "Show's over, folks. Go on about your business."

The crowd slowly broke up and moved along. Laura couldn't decide if the sheriff's appearance would help or hinder them. If Francesca told them something important, Laura wanted the sheriff to hear her. But Francesca had been about to break, and she might become more determined to keep her secret with the sheriff to back her.

Three minutes later Laura, Chase, Francesca and the sheriff were back in the station house. The sheriff looked at Chase, his expression thoughtful. "Tell me what's going on here. Why're you harassing my employee?"

"Francesca told us she was with a lover at the time someone was shooting at us—but she lied. Her hair's the same color as Laura's. And she also knew that Brent died from stab wounds to the throat. Now how would she know that if she wasn't there?"

"I told you—" Francesca leaned forward, her hands clasping the sheriff's. Laura lost track of the conversation as a gleaming ruby-and-gold ring on a chain around Francesca's neck swung forward.

Ruby red. Winking at her.

Oh, God! She'd seen that ring before—around Brent Sutton's neck the night he died.

Without asking permission, Laura plucked the ring and chain from Francesca's neck. She turned it back and forth, examining the stone and band. Yes! She was sure it was the same ring. The implications tumbled through her mind while exhilaration rushed through her veins.

"Hey!" Francesca objected, face flushing, voice strident. "That's my grandfather's ring."

Unable to contain her excitement, Laura rose to her feet and glared at Francesca. "And why was your grandfather's ring around Brent's neck the night he died?"

Chase's eyes glinted with light, like the sun breaking through a late-afternoon fog. Laura could feel hope and intensity radiating from him, warming her, fueling her with the additional strength to keep pushing for answers.

The sheriff frowned at Laura, but for the first time, she sensed he was taking her seriously. "What are you talking about?"

Laura licked her bottom lip, pausing to make the right words come out of her dry mouth. She held out the distinctive ring and let it swing and catch the light. "The night Brent attacked me, he was wearing this ring on a chain around his neck."

"Th-that's ridiculous," Francesca stuttered, her face going ashen. "My grandfather gave me that ring. His initials are engraved on the band with a date."

The sheriff frowned, the ridges of his brows drawn into a frustrated line. "That ring wasn't around Brent's neck when we staked out the crime scene."

"That's because the killer removed it." Laura pointed at Francesca. "She didn't want to leave a clue to her identity and the initials engraved in the band would have led you straight to her."

"Her mother works for my father," Chase said adding up the circumstantial evidence. "Francesca often rode a horse kept in the stable."

Francesca shook her head with the wildness of an untamed mare with a lasso's loop closing around her neck. "You have no proof! She's making up a story and accusing me so you'll drop the charges against her."

Laura winced at Francesca's words, recognizing the truth in them. She still didn't have any proof unless the hair sample at Tyler's murder scene turned out to be Francesca's. It was still Laura's fingerprints alone on the murder weapon. They had caught Francesca but they needed to tighten the noose and jerk the woman to her knees until she confessed, only Laura didn't have a clue how to do it.

Chase delivered the words that would set her free. "There *is* proof. I saw Brent wear the ring and so did Tyler."

"Excuse me, but Tyler can't back up your story from the grave," the sheriff pointed out.

"But the Senator can." Chase's voice warmed with victory. "He once asked Brent about the ring over dinner, teased him about going steady with a town girl."

"He'd lie to protect the mother of his grandson," Francesca objected, fighting like a downed mare as the loops were tied around her hooves to prevent any chance of escape.

"And—" Chase's eyes sparkled as he caught and held Laura's gaze "—we have a picture over the mantel of Brent wearing it."

Francesca's shoulders slumped at Chase's words. Her head sagged and her chest heaved bitter sobs. "I knew no one would believe me."

The sheriff scratched his chin, looking from Laura and Chase to Francesca. He might have believed Laura guilty, but after hearing the evidence against Francesca Martin, he could no longer avoid the truth. "Ms. Martin, you're under arrest. You have the right to remain silent. You have the right to an attorney. If you can't afford council, the court will appoint an attorney for you. Do you understand these rights?"

A whole future suddenly opened in front of Laura. Chase and Keith and her, together. She would have her world back. Her freedom. Almost overwhelmed with happiness and relief, she had trouble following the conversation still going on in the room around her.

While Laura ached to dance with joy, Francesca hung her head. Her voice came out a broken whisper. "I want to cooperate. I'll tell you everything. But you won't believe me."

The sheriff cuffed her hands behind her back. "Try me."

"Brent Sutton raped me." She raised her chin with defiance. "He took my granddaddy's ring as a trophy to remind me he could take me again whenever he wanted."

The sheriff scratched his head, obviously doubting her story. "Excuse me, but I'm confused. You were in the barn when Brent Sutton attacked Ms. Embry?"

"I'd been out riding my mother's horse, wearing gloves." So that's why Laura's were the only prints on the pitchfork. "Brent came in drunk and I hid so he couldn't hurt me again."

"Again? When did he rape you?" Laura asked, believing the dispatcher's story. She'd seen the wild look in Brent's eyes that night, heard his incriminating intentions from his own lips. If not for luck and the handy pitchfork, Brent might have hurt her, too. And while she felt sorry for Francesca, she couldn't quite forgive her for allowing Laura to take the murder rap.

"That afternoon before Brent died, he caught me without my gun while I hosed down Mom's mare.

Afterward, I ran away but I had to go back for my car. That's when I saw Brent go after you.''

''Why didn't you tell someone?'' the sheriff asked, tapping his pen as he wrote down details on a pad of paper.

''Who would believe me? A poor town girl's word against the Senator's son, the heir to the Sutton fortune? Mom would have lost her job. And you wouldn't have hired me.''

Francesca's words struck home. Laura hadn't come forward for the same reasons Francesca hadn't.

''You heard everything?'' Laura asked, already knowing the answer but needing to hear confirmation.

''I thought you'd killed the SOB—wish you had,'' Francesca said to Laura. ''But after you left, he staggered to his feet, swearing a blue streak and I stabbed him with the pitchfork.''

''Did he attack you first?'' The sheriff asked.

''Don't answer that question,'' Laura advised, feeling sorry for the woman in spite of what she'd done.

''He was so angry, cursing and violent. I was so scared, I couldn't think straight. So I picked up the pitchfork and stabbed him. I watched his life blood run into the straw. And I was glad he was dead and couldn't hurt me again.''

Laura tried to steal herself against sympathizing with Francesca's predicament. But it wasn't easy.

''Did you shoot at Laura and Chase as they drove into town?'' Clearly the sheriff had no compunction about wanting all the details cleared up.

''That wasn't me.''

"Really." Chase folded his arms over his chest. "Then where were you that day?"

"At the bank."

Chase cocked his brow. "That sounds like another lie."

Francesca sighed. "I didn't want you to know because I pulled out all my money."

In case things went wrong, Laura thought. Francesca had been preparing to run away.

"You knew emptying your account would look suspicious," the sheriff said.

"I have a withdrawal slip in my purse," Francesca said, "see for yourself. The time is stamped on the slip somewhere."

With a sinking feeling in her gut, Laura found the slip. "It's dated for last Thursday and the time is 3:10 p.m." The withdrawal slip confirmed that Francesca couldn't have been at the bank and shooting at them at the same time. What the hell was going on?

"Did you kill Tyler, too?" The sheriff asked.

Francesca shook her head. "Why would I kill Tyler? He was always kind to me."

Chase and Laura exchanged a long look. Could it be possible there was another killer on the loose? They'd never really considered the possibility of two killers, both trying to frame her. The circumstances couldn't just be coincidence, two murderers, attacking two brothers, both blaming Laura. Impossible. And yet, the slip of paper in her hand mocked her.

"How do we know you aren't lying about Tyler, like you did before?" Noel asked.

"It doesn't matter now. I no longer have a reason

to lie about Tyler since I'll be spending the rest of my life in jail for killing Brent."

Chase's hands closed into fists. "You have any idea why someone wanted Tyler dead?"

A faraway look came into Francesca's eyes. "I once overheard Brent and the Senator talking about evidence at the courthouse—that if the secret got out it would destroy everyone."

Another clue that maybe the Senator and his family had an enemy? Or was Laura once again being suspicious for no good reason?

"What kind of secret?" Chase asked.

"That's all I heard, sorry." Francesca turned and faced Laura. "If it means anything to you, I'm sorry you took the blame. I never expected that to happen."

"Noel." The sheriff's secretary came over to him, a piece of paper in her hand. "I thought you'd want to see this fax right away."

The sheriff scanned the paper and looked up. "This is the DNA test on the hair sample we found. The Senator must have pulled some strings for it to come back so fast."

Laura tensed, praying for good news. If the hair turned out to be Francesca's, Laura would be cleared of all wrongdoing. From the look on the sheriff's face, she couldn't even hazard a guess at the results.

Laura held her breath. She'd just been cleared of one murder. Was it too much to hope that the storm clouds hanging over her head would vanish?

"And...?" Chase prodded, irritation warring with impatience at the sheriff's leaving them hanging.

The sheriff let out an irritated sigh. "I'm sorry. It's a positive match for Ms. Embry."

WHILE CHASE INSISTED that the sheriff couldn't arrest Laura for Tyler's murder, she'd seemed to take the new evidence against her with unnerving calm, almost as if she'd been expecting bad news. He couldn't put her through another arrest, another bail hearing, especially since Tyler was alive. But he couldn't explain to the sheriff, either—not without breaking his word to the Senator.

Francesca's confession had thrown Chase's thoughts into a tailspin, and while he was grateful Laura had been cleared of one murder, he needed to protect her from a second arrest. So he'd called a family meeting, knowing he could count on his brothers' commitment against a common enemy. They would all pull together and the Sutton strength would defeat the enemy.

Unfortunately the sheriff had insisted on following Chase and Laura to the Sutton ranch, claiming that Brent's picture over the mantel with Francesca's ring around his neck was evidence. Chase and Laura didn't speak on the ride to the ranch since Chase had to phone each brother and call them in from work.

The Senator canceled his appointments and delayed his flight. Cameron didn't say a word of complaint at having his fishing cut short. Rafe had agreed to meet them in half an hour.

"Maybe I should have Bradley join us," Laura suggested from beside Chase. She'd scooted to the middle of the seat and rested her head on his shoulder, her golden-blond hair cascading onto his chest like rays of sunshine.

He thought of Tyler and shook his head. "Let's wait on that."

"Why?" She looked over at him, her finely arched brows drawing together in a slight frown.

Chase hated steering her in the wrong direction. He didn't like lies or evading her answer with silence. Soon. Soon, he promised himself, he'd be free to tell her, but a cold nagging knot formed when he considered whether she'd ever forgive him. "Bradley might not like that we suspected his secretary Sally of murder. Not when he's about to marry her after having been a widower for so many years."

Chase placed an arm over Laura's shoulder, and she snuggled against his side, her hand resting lightly on his thigh. "I can imagine nothing worse than losing a wife and two children, Bradley's entire family. That poor man deserves to find happiness with someone else and Sally certainly appears to love him."

Chase would never tire of holding Laura next to him, breathing in the scent of her hair, feeling the softness of her skin, listening to her thoughtful words. He wanted to spend the rest of his life with this woman, have more children together in this gorgeous land.

Chase never tired of the drive from the public road onto Sutton land that followed a ridge that hid the main house from first view. The road made a gradual ascent to the north, passed a brow of massive cliffs that had been dynamited to clear a path into the rolling valley where the Senator had built his home.

The house, although huge in size, was not imposing and the design had a natural fluidity with a majesty that matched the vast lands and towering mountains that surrounded it. Solid rock walls, giant picture windows with stunning views of the spectacular scenery lent an elegance to a house that he thought of as an enduring monument to the future. The long drive swept around an elegant curve that brought visitors up under arching boughs of transplanted oaks that was more reminiscent of the Old South than the West. Yet, the house was built with massive stone fireplaces and steeply pitched hip roofs to ward off the cold and weight of Colorado winter snows.

Chase parked and noticed Laura bracing her shoulders and lifting her chin with pride. He took her hand and squeezed. "My father is on our side."

"If you say so."

The sheriff parked his car just as Rafe, tires squealing, veered a golf cart around the corner of the house. Speed was Rafe's best friend and no matter what he rode, trucks, cars, horses, bulls or golf carts, he always pushed the limit. Without waiting for the cart to roll to a stop, Rafe leapt out like a graceful gazelle and greeted them with a jaunty wave. "What's up?"

"I ought to issue you a ticket," the sheriff said as he held out his hand for Rafe to shake.

Cam, driving a four-wheel-drive Jeep, kicked up dust as he drove in at a much more deliberate pace, followed by the Senator in his limousine. Cam waited for the Senator and then the two men approached the group, offering their hands first to Laura in greeting. They all settled in the Senator's library, Laura beside Chase on a leather sofa of topgrain hide soft enough to snuggle into and put one at ease. But one look at Laura chewing her bottom lip gave away her nervousness.

Rafe straddled an antique chair, tilting it back so he balanced like a cat on just the spindly rear legs. Cam folded meaty but muscular arms over his chest and waited with a patience none of the other brothers had while the Senator told his aide that he would be unavailable to take calls until further notice.

The sheriff removed Brent's picture from the mantel and departed. After everyone refused refreshments, Chase recapped Francesca's confession and concluded with the DNA hair sample matching Laura's.

No one interrupted and when Chase finished, Rafe let out a long, low whistle. "So you're saying Tyler's murderer is still out there?"

"Maybe this is a conspiracy against our family," the Senator suggested.

Chase looked at his father. "Francesca said she overheard you talking to Brent about courthouse records that had to remain a secret."

The Senator's expression didn't change. "That couldn't have anything to do with what's happening now."

Cam didn't move or fidget but his brilliant mind would be turning over the facts, examining every detail in the same way he examined medical charts for clues and diagnosed patients with remarkable accuracy. "Maybe someone is taking advantage of the circumstances."

"What do you mean?" Laura spoke up and Chase was glad she felt free to do so. He wanted her to feel comfortable with his family.

"I'm just hypothesizing, mind you," Cam spoke slowly but his thoughts could move at lightning speed. "Maybe Francesca wasn't part of a conspiracy, but I don't believe the murders were a coincidence. That only leaves a few possibilities."

"Like what?" Rafe asked.

"Suppose someone thought they could get away with murdering Tyler by placing the blame on Laura? After all, everyone thought Laura killed Brent. Why not make it appear as if she'd killed Tyler, too?"

"Only I didn't kill Brent," Laura said.

"Exactly." Cam nodded, the thick cords in his neck tensed, his gray eyes stormy. "The killer made a mistake by planting Laura's hair instead of Francesca's at the scene of Tyler's accident."

"This theory is pretty far-out there," Rafe said with a rakish grimace, "even for you, Cam."

The Senator took out a cigar and rolled it between his fingers. "Well, Cam's theory fits unless you want to go with the fluke theory. And if you believe that, I have a three-legged racehorse I'd like to sell you."

"Well, there are other possibilities, too," Cam admitted. "Perhaps the murders have to do with our missing cattle. By Rafe's count, we're short a few hundred head. But neither rustling nor a conspiracy theory makes sense unless Francesca was working for someone—and I doubt that."

Chase frowned. "And if the killer didn't set up Laura for Tyler's death out of malice, there'd be no point. She'd already been arrested for one murder, setting her up for a second murder would be pointless if they just wanted revenge against Laura."

The Senator unwrapped his cigar. "Which is what I've thought for some time. Someone killed Brent, went after Tyler. And now they want Chase dead, too. Cam might be the next target."

Cam glared at Chase as if he'd take it as a personal insult if the killer got him. "Maybe we should hire Chase a full-time bodyguard."

Chase narrowed his eyes. "Look, I want to draw the sucker out, not send him into hiding."

The library door opened suddenly. At the unexpected interruption, every head turned toward the disturbance. Tyler, back from a week of eternal sleep, limped in, wearing a bandage around his forehead, leaning on his cane and a cocky grin plastered above a newly grown beard. Clearly out of his coma, he was very much alive.

Elation washed over Chase with a roaring wave. But when he came up for air and took in Laura's stricken look, he knew he was drowning. As Rafe clapped Tyler on the back and Cam carried over a chair for Tyler to sit on, Laura gasped.

"You're supposed to be dead!"

The Senator clamped down on his cigar. "That's right. You're *supposed* to be dead. What are you doing here?"

Tyler shrugged. "You made up that story to protect me when I was in a coma. Now that I'm awake, I can defend myself. And I'm not about to hide when this family is having a crisis."

Laura trembled. "Oh, God! You're alive."

Her body braced as though against a bullet, her eyes molten with the beginnings of rage, happiness and confusion, she turned to Chase, her face stricken. "Tyler's alive."

The Senator hugged his son, tears in his eyes. "It's good to have you home."

The corners of Tyler's mouth turned up higher in a pale-faced grin. "I wanted to surprise you."

"The doctor gave you permission to leave the hospital?" Cam asked.

"Ever since I woke up two days ago, they've poked and prodded and tested me. Except for some minor neurological damage to the nerves in my leg I'm fine." Tyler held up his cane. "The nurses said I looked dashing with the cane, but I don't expect to need it much longer."

"Can you remember what happened?" Chase asked, praying his brother could name his attacker.

"Not a bloody thing. The doctors said short-term memory loss is normal for this kind of accident."

Laura rose to her feet, her entire body trembling, her eyes damning Chase. And even as she raged at him, he couldn't deny her courage or her style. "Damn it. You told me he was dead. You had his funeral. You lied to me and kept right on lying when I had been accused of his murder. And all along he was in a coma?"

Chase wished he could take the pain he'd caused her inside himself. She was fighting tears, outraged and betrayed, and he had done this to her.

Her voice shook. "You didn't trust me."

"I'm sorry." He reached for her and she jerked back. "I don't know what to say."

"There's nothing you can say."

The Senator moved from Tyler's side to stand next to Chase. "Laura, Chase wanted to tell you but I made him promise to remain silent."

"Obviously his loyalty to you is stronger than what he feels for me. No doubt you are very proud of him." Pain radiated from her voice.

"Tyler was barely hanging on. His life was at stake."

"And so was mine, Senator." Chase had never been prouder of her as she stood up to his father with such dignity, nor had he ever been as frightened by what he might lose if she left him. Blond hair cascaded over her shoulders like an angry waterfall. Her blue eyes were a dark, stormy sea. "You let everyone think I murdered your sons. I could have been sent to jail. How dare you?"

"I wouldn't have let the deception go that far. Tyler was helpless and unconscious. I needed to protect my son from a killer and the best way to do that was to make the killer think he'd succeeded the first time."

Laura's eyes turned glacial blue, her voice frosty. "And while you were protecting your son, you let the world believe I was a murderer." She turned away from the Senator and glared at Chase with horror and tears and disbelief that he'd gone along with the deception. "And you kept his secret? You didn't trust me enough to tell me the truth?"

Fueled by fear that he could lose her forever, his voice grew harsh. "Let me refresh your memory. Who ran away for two years because she could not trust me? Who hid my son from me?"

Her lashes swept up, revealing eyes sheened bright with angry tears. "I was smarter then than I am now," she conceded, wounding him with her pain.

"Chase lied because he loves me," Tyler said in an attempt to defend the deception.

From the set of her jaw and the furious line of her lips, Chase knew words of reason weren't going to sway her. Laura's long legs ate up the distance to the door in angry steps. "If that's the kind of love that holds this family together, I don't want any part of it."

The door slammed behind her, leaving Chase's feet rooted to the floor, his heart trampled. She'd left him and he'd deserved every angry word she'd said to him. He'd hurt her deeply, betrayed her trust and she wouldn't forgive him. He'd lost her. And still he burned for her. Wanting her with every breath he drew while she despised him would be his punishment. He would have preferred to be flayed alive rather than to have hurt her so.

"What are you waiting for, boy?" the Senator used his most persuasive roar.

Chase lifted his head. "Huh?"

"Go after her, son."

"She doesn't want me."

"She wouldn't have been so hurt if she didn't want you," Cam told him wisely.

"Go talk to her," Tyler urged, waving him toward the door with his cane.

"She won't listen."

"Hell," Rafe swore. "Any fool can see you're bigger than she is. Just pick her up and kiss her senseless until she changes her mind."

Chapter Eleven

Laura should have enjoyed watching her angry words wound Chase like bullets. After his lies, she should have enjoyed watching him bleed inside. But even if she'd had a knife in her hand, she couldn't have sliced out his heart, because, damn him, he didn't have one. At least not where she was concerned.

Stumbling over small rocks that bordered the garden, Laura fled toward the Embry ranch. She wanted to go home and hold her son, rock him on her lap and curse the man who had spurned her love. Chase had had no right to make love to her so tenderly and then lie to her. Damn him! He had no right to make her want him.

She'd made a perfectly good life for herself and her son. And she hadn't wanted to return to see what she would miss if she ended up in jail. But Chase had pushed and prodded and made promises with his hands and mouth and eyes until she would have done anything he asked. And look where loving him had gotten her? Used. Betrayed. Wanting what she could never have.

Chase.

Miserable cur. He'd proven where she stood in his eyes. She'd never be as good as the almighty Suttons. When it came down to making decisions, she'd always be chosen last. She didn't belong in his family. She wasn't good enough to be told the truth, and the thought stung.

Clearing the garden, she raced across open pasture, pumping her legs and arms, trying to run away from angry thoughts. She welcomed the burning pain in her legs that would never match the fire of hurt in her heart.

Why had he walked back into her life? She'd been over him, mostly. And then he'd found her, stuck with her and gave her hope, until she'd let down her guard. He'd become her whole world. She thought of Chase when she awakened in the morning and when she went to sleep at night. And in between, she saw his face in her child during every waking minute. She'd opened her heart, her body, her soul to him.

And that's when he'd zapped her, slicing her up, shredding her into frayed ribbons left scattered in a storm until she barely knew where her pain started and her flesh stopped. Damn him for making her love him. Damn him for giving her hope and then destroying it with a ruthlessness that had left her feeling sick and weary and tired.

She scrambled across the pasture, picking the most direct route to Embry land. Instinct caused her to glance over her shoulder. Chase was coming after her and a prickle of alarm tightened her neck. She forced tired legs faster, avoiding ruts and hollows, pushing her burning lungs until her breath came in ragged gasps and her muscles burned. She didn't glance back, couldn't afford to lose a second, but she could hear him gaining on her.

"Laura! Please…stop."

She was no match for his speed, slowed and faced him with her hands resting on her hips. "What?"

Barely breathing hard, he skidded to a halt. "Are you okay?"

She might never be okay again. Despite the verdant pastures beneath her feet and clear skies overhead, her world tilted out of kilter. Pride made her voice strong. "I want to go home."

"Home is where your heart is and your heart belongs to me." He held his arms open, beckoning to her. In the last rays of sunlight, he appeared a mighty warrior expecting welcome after battle and she wanted nothing more than to step into his arms, to take comfort in his strength. But she wouldn't be able to face herself in the mirror if she did.

Swallowing the lump in her throat, she turned away from him, but not before watching his eyes darken to gun metal gray, not before seeing his large fingers clench and unclench with frustration.

"Laura, I don't want to lose you."

She spoke between tattered breaths of anger. "You should have thought of that before you lied to me."

"I figured our love was strong enough to withstand a few lies."

"You figured wrong."

"Did I?" The agony in his tone kept her from walking away. "I forgave you for keeping my son from me. Can't you forgive me?"

"I don't know." Incredible pain tore at her soul and as much as she would've liked to have gone on with their relationship and pretended he hadn't lied to her, she couldn't. What he'd done had been deliberate, a well-orchestrated plan, involving his entire family.

While her running away from Colorado had come from panic. Perhaps they didn't deserve to love since they apparently couldn't trust one another. Maybe they didn't love at all, perhaps what she felt was only lust. But even in her wrenching pain, she knew better. She'd wanted Chase Sutton with her whole heart.

As if sensing her indecision, Chase took her hand, his voice low and pleading. "Talk to me."

Her throat tightened on bitter tears she refused to shed and almost made her choke. "I can't."

"I know you're furious and hurting. I…made a mistake and I'm sorry."

"We've both made mistakes," she agreed, but she didn't know if she could get past them. "Perhaps, we aren't supposed to be together."

"Or perhaps we are and this is only a test to gauge the depth of our feelings." He took both her hands in his, infusing her with heat. "We have a son. We need to make an effort for him."

Her heart lurched with regret and fears. "Is that why you want me? Because we have a son."

"That's not why I wanted you the first time and that's not why I want you now. But your having Keith made it easier for me to forgive you for running away," he admitted with the honesty she'd always admired.

Heart troubled, she looked deep into his eyes, knowing he wanted an answer, deserved an answer.

She didn't know whether she could be so forgiving. How could she ever trust him again?

"Tell me what you're thinking," he urged.

"I need time."

"Take all you need. I'll be here for you. Waiting." Chase's cell phone rang and he answered it without taking his gaze from hers. "Yes?"

He leaned over and tilted the phone to her ear so she could hear the conversation. "Laura's with me."

"Good," the Senator's distinctive drawl came across the line. "I thought you should know that Bradley didn't leave court at three o'clock the day those shots were fired at you."

Her attorney had lied? Why?

"Bradley may have had a meeting with Judge Stewart that he didn't want to advertise." Judge Stewart, her grandfather's old friend, had paid her bail. As a prominent citizen, it wasn't odd that his name kept turning up in their questioning of other suspects, but she couldn't contain her suspicions. "My sources can't pinpoint his location at three o'clock that day but I thought you should know he wasn't where he claimed to be."

"Thanks, Dad."

"Oh, and one more thing. Lance signed for a delivery of a part at three-fifteen that day."

While Laura appreciated that Chase had shared the phone message with her, she didn't automatically believe he trusted her. Her nerves were too raw and she didn't trust her own judgment any more than she trusted Chase. But after the harsh words she'd spoken to the Senator, she was relieved he still intended to help them.

While she could no longer be pinned with Tyler's murder, the district attorney could still charge her with attempted homicide. With the Senator on her side, the authorities might not even bring her to trial. Yet she couldn't just walk away. Not with Chase's life still in danger. He'd stood by her when she needed him and now she would do the same for him. Later, when she'd had time to calm down and think things through, she'd decide if they had a future together.

THE FOLLOWING MORNING, Chase had wanted to confront Bradley about his whereabouts the day he and Laura had been shot at. But Laura insisted they go to the courthouse. With their relationship on tenuous ground, he hadn't argued.

Laura had gone from warm and open to frosty and remote. While she wasn't rude, she wasn't sharing her thoughts. Clearly she was still deeply troubled by his lie.

Chase could only blame himself. He'd known she was innocent. Known she was trustworthy. But his actions hadn't reflected his beliefs, and he wondered if he'd destroyed the special closeness they'd had.

They entered the musty-smelling courthouse and bumped into the sheriff who stood talking to Judge Stewart. The men greeted them and again Laura took the opportunity to thank Judge Stewart for putting up her bail. "It was kind of you, sir."

The judge accepted her thanks like a strutting peacock. "I knew Embry's granddaughter couldn't have been a murderer."

"How so?" asked the sheriff.

"She has good blood."

"I thank you for believing in me," Laura said, her voice warm. "And I was wondering…"

"Yes?" the judge asked, and Chase realized she'd neatly maneuvered him into answering her questions.

"Were you with my attorney last Thursday around three o'clock?"

Judge Stewart scratched his head. "I can't recall. If you phone my secretary she might be able to tell you."

Laura shook the judge's hand and then kissed him on the cheek. "Thanks again, you've been a great help, sir."

While Laura's smooth questions might have fooled the judge, the sheriff eyed them with a bit more curiosity than Chase deemed necessary. "What are you two doing here?"

"Getting a marriage license," Chase lied and slid his arm over Laura's shoulder. Although Laura's eyes darted to his with questions, she didn't openly contradict him.

The sheriff broke into a genuine grin and clapped Chase on the back. "Congratulations! Have you set a date?"

"Not yet." Laura plastered a smile on her lips that never reached her eyes. "We're taking this one step at a time."

"I'd be happy to perform the ceremony," Judge Stewart offered.

"You're very kind." As Laura made polite conversation, Chase noted how the sheriff's attitude had changed. Where once he'd been sarcastic and aloof, he'd now had a drastic change of heart. No doubt the sheriff took his cue from the Senator and didn't care to offend Chase's powerful father. And to give the man credit, he no longer suspected Laura of murder.

Chase and Laura continued along the hall and she dug her elbow into his ribs. He let go of her. "Ow! Careful!"

"I should smack you up the side of your head," she threatened, but the chuckle in her voice gave away her true feelings. "Did you have to say we were getting married?"

"I didn't want to tell them the truth and considering where we are," he gestured to the courthouse, "that's the first thing that popped into my head."

"For heaven's sake! I can't take you anywhere. Why didn't you just say we were checking a tax bill? Or needed a legal description?"

Chase shrugged, trying to contain his impatience. As far as he was concerned he was humoring her wild-goose chase to look through old documents, but their relationship was too rocky to say so. And since he preferred her teasing to her giving him the cold shoulder, he didn't complain too much. "I'm not even sure what we're doing here."

"I want a look around. Both ranches are losing cattle to rustlers. Dad told me this morning we're missing over three hundred head. And I can't forget that Francesca overheard Brent and the Senator talking about a secret at the courthouse. We should probably check birth and death records, maybe marriage records, too. But the most valuable thing around here is land ownership. Why don't we check the plat maps, move on to the tax records and if nothing shows up try the more personal records?"

"Sounds good."

She seemed determined to uncover his father's old secret, clearly didn't trust the Senator, and Chase wondered if the breach could ever be mended. One step at a time. First she would have to forgive him before she forgave the rest of the family.

The Sutton ranch was too large to fit onto a page of one plat book. But that didn't faze Laura. She sat turning the pages, paying particular attention to the shared property lines between the Embry and Sutton ranches.

After twenty minutes, Chase sighed and tried to keep the frustration from his tone. "You think these maps will tell you where to find missing cattle?"

"See these old photographs?" She pointed to the top parts of the map which were actual black-and-white aerial pictures of the site. "Our wild ride down the train track gave me an idea. Part of our route seemed to be an old trail. I'm hoping to find an old dirt road, something that's been closed for years."

"And what could be the possible connection between stolen cattle and my father's secret?"

"Maybe there isn't one. But you're the man who said we should check every clue." She rubbed the back of her neck and he longed to replace her fingers with his own but suspected she would pull away. Rather then let her reject his touch, he'd wait until she was ready. He'd told her he'd give her time. He just hadn't realized following through would be so hard.

His fingers itched to caress her silky blond hair, knead the muscles in her delicate neck, nibble a path over skin as soft as a kitten's whiskers. At the thought of touching her, his blood surged and his jeans became uncomfortably tight.

"Look!" Laura turned the plat book's page and pointed excitedly.

He leaned over her shoulder, taking in a whiff of her freshly washed hair, then forced his eyes to focus. She was pointing to ten prime acres of land.

"So?"

Her voice rose with excitement. "This piece has a different folio number."

Chase knew folio numbers identified sections of land for tax purposes. But he could see no reason for her excitement. "Lots of sections have different folio numbers. So what?"

"This piece is much smaller than the others. It's only ten acres. All the other folio numbers on the Sutton spread refer to hundred-acre parcels."

"And the significance is?"

"This piece was clearly once part of the Sutton acreage. Now it is held by a different owner."

"How do you know?"

"By the tract size." She pointed. "See—all the other parcels are hundred-acre tracts. But this one is only a few acres."

"Are you saying a Sutton sold it or bought it?"

"It wasn't bought separately because—"

"The Senator bought the property in one piece." The significance of her find had him puzzled. "And Dad has always sworn not to break up the land. He wouldn't even sell three acres he owns on the far side of the road to those condo developers."

"Exactly." Laura copied the folio number on a piece of paper. "Come on."

"Now where are we going?" Chase was no longer complaining.

"To where the county keeps the deeds. I want to see who owns this piece of land."

Ten minutes later, Laura had pulled up the files and looked through a view screen at recorded deeds. "The land has been dedicated to the county for a park."

"A park on Sutton land? I wonder why Dad never—"

"Your father didn't donate the land to the park. Mark Bradley did."

"You mean Bradley handled the paperwork?"

"Hold on." Laura scanned through additional files. "Twenty years ago your father gave the land to Bradley, and the attorney donated the property to the county."

"I don't understand." His father donated money to charity but he always held on to the land. He'd drilled into his sons that the ranch must be kept intact and under no circumstances should the land be mortgaged or sold. Chase reluctantly reached for his cell phone. "I'll ask the Senator."

"I have a better idea. Let's go talk to Bradley."

"I still think the Senator should be there. Is that okay with you?"

LAURA WAS AMAZED at how quickly Chase got everyone together. They all met in Bradley's conference room, the Senator, Tyler, Cam, Chase, Rafe and Laura. While she wondered why the entire Sutton clan had shown up, she didn't question their right to be there. She was convinced someone was trying to kill the Sutton sons and Suttons stuck together. Maybe she could put all their brains to good use.

When Tyler limped in, Bradley's eyes opened wide in astonishment. "You're alive!"

Tyler settled into a chair, trying to disguise a wince of pain. "Yep."

Bradley caught on to the ruse immediately and saluted the Senator. "Very smooth. And now the D.A. will drop the murder charges against Laura."

"I'd wanted to keep Tyler's recovery a secret just a little longer, but he had other ideas," the Senator announced. "But I'd still feel better if tomorrow Chase, Laura and Tyler searched the high pastures for our missing cattle and kept out of sight."

"You have an idea who's after your family?" Bradley asked with the acute intelligence of a crack attorney who'd put pieces together within the space of a heartbeat.

The Senator shook his head. "They should be safe enough up there until we figure out the particulars."

Bradley tapped his pencil impatiently. Before Laura or Chase could bring up their own questions concerning Bradley's whereabouts on the day of the shooting or the land parcel he'd donated to the county, Bradley brought up a new concern. "I believe there's something you all should know." He focused on the Senator. "Well, something the Senator already knows but prefers to keep hidden."

His sons gave their father curious looks. Laura held her breath.

The Senator helped himself to a glass of water off the sideboard. Tall, commanding and relaxed, he looked as if he hadn't a care in the world—not a man worried about his family. With all eyes on him, he sure knew how to play a crowd. ''I'm waiting with bated breath.''

''Your wife, Genia, had a tough first pregnancy,'' Bradley stated. The Senator stiffened at the mention of his deceased wife as the attorney continued. ''The baby died.''

Chase sucked in his breath with a hiss. Cam didn't move while Rafe tilted back his chair on two legs and rocked. Laura thought that everyone was acting strangely and wondered if the brothers already knew what Bradley was about to say.

Tyler threaded fingers through his ragged hair. ''I fail to see—''

''You will.'' Bradley paused and cleared his throat, seemingly enjoying the tension. ''Genia almost died along with the baby, and was in and out of consciousness for weeks. The Senator couldn't tell his precious wife that their son had died.'' He sipped from his glass and no one said a word. ''During that time, another woman gave birth in the same hospital, intending to give the baby up for adoption.''

''What are you saying?'' Chase asked and from his astounded expression Laura knew the Senator had kept some secrets from his own family.

''The Senator adopted a child, Brent, substituting him for the baby that died.''

Tyler jumped to his feet, his fists clenched. ''What?''

For an instant, Laura thought she saw genuine anger mixed with bleak grief on the Senator's face. Then the mask returned, cool and polished, belying what she'd seen. Bradley's announcement had seemed to come out of nowhere. She didn't understand where her attorney was going with this old information but clearly he was taking too much pleasure in telling them about the Senator's past.

The Senator's voice held a hard edge. "How did you find out?"

Bradley couldn't contain the lilt of triumph in his tone or the light in his eyes. "A good attorney has his sources."

While his sons reeled from the news, the Senator faced the man across the table with a frosty fury. "There's no law against adoption."

Bradley almost smirked. "Then you won't mind the facts of Brent's birth becoming public?"

Laura was baffled. What was Bradley's motivation for threatening the Senator with an old scandal? Who would care that the Senator had adopted a son and chosen to keep the news private? If Bradley thought the Sutton sons wouldn't rally around their father, then the attorney had badly misjudged the family.

Chase ignored the attorney, his eyes on his father. "Brent wasn't our biological brother?"

"But he looked like us," Rafe insisted.

"Not really." The Senator sighed. "He had dark hair and dark eyes. And he was a troubled man with a drinking problem and a violent streak. People see what they want to see."

"Mother never suspected?" Chase asked.

"If she did, she never mentioned it to me."

"Dad, it doesn't matter." Cam rose and squeezed the Senator's shoulder. "Brent was our brother in all the ways that matter."

Tyler's voice shook. "And his parentage doesn't change the fact that Francesca killed him."

Puzzled more by the reason Bradley had told the story than by what he'd uncovered, Laura shifted uneasily in her chair. Bradley must know the Senator preferred to keep his family business private. And he had to realize how much it would cost the proud Senator to have a decades-old secret revealed by the press, his good name smeared by the paparazzi.

In the tense silence that followed Bradley's stunning revelation, Laura commented, "I don't see what a twenty-eight-year-old adoption has to do with figuring out who almost murdered Tyler and who shot at us."

Bradley tapped his pencil until the Suttons stilled and he regained their attention. "Francesca killed Brent but she says she didn't go after Tyler or Chase." He swiveled in his chair and directed his comments to the Senator. "But someone is trying to kill your sons, Senator. It seems to me, Brent's biological parents have a perfect motive. You gave their son too much responsibility and he turned into a violent alcoholic that led to his death. Maybe they want revenge."

Chase's eyes narrowed to slits but he remained silent, his muscles tensed like a cougar about to spring on prey.

Rafe stood so fast his chair banged the floor. "That's preposterous!"

Tyler slammed his cane on the table. "Outrageous."

Cam looked more thoughtful than angry but his

huge muscles contracted as if he were holding himself still with great control.

The Senator remained cool under pressure. "Brent's biological mother died of cancer over fifteen years ago. She never revealed who fathered the child, wouldn't even say if the man knew she'd brought Brent into the world. And in all these years, the father's never come forward, so it's unlikely he'd suddenly want revenge for the death of his son. But, of course, the press will go bonkers over the story." The Senator's eyes drilled Bradley's, and not for the first time, Laura thought that these two men had some unresolved differences. "Somehow I don't think it's Brent's biological father who wants revenge."

Was the Senator implying Bradley wanted revenge and he'd told the Sutton sons this story out of spite? Laura actually felt sorry for the Senator. She supposed that if Bradley hadn't uncovered the truth about the adoption, the Senator would have taken the secret to his grave. And she certainly couldn't fault the man for loving his troubled adopted son as much as his biological ones—he'd been ready to leave Brent in charge of his most prized possession, the Sutton ranch.

The Senator had loved his family, protected his wife against the knowledge their own son had died and adopted a stranger's child to love. The Senator's motives had been honorable and yet she imagined the press would twist and turn the truth, dragging the Sutton name through the mud.

Laura frowned. "I don't see why the press must be informed."

Bradley slapped a tabloid onto the conference table. "They already know."

At the gleam of malice in Bradley's eyes, Laura wondered if he had informed the press. But what would he have to gain?

The Senator's back stiffened and he turned one palm up and spoke to his sons. "This is old news and will blow over. We've weathered worse storms and we'll sail through this one. I'm more concerned over finding out who wants to destroy my family than any bad publicity."

Laura couldn't help admiring the man who cared more about his family than bad press—the country needed more politicians like him in Washington. In the aching silence, she wanted to change the subject smoothly but didn't know how. So she just blurted out her question to her attorney. "Bradley, you told us you were in court until three o'clock on the day someone shot at us. But that's not true. Why did you lie?"

"Because I didn't want to admit where I really was."

"And where was that?" Chase asked.

"Judge Stewart and I…went hunting."

Chapter Twelve

The Senator ushered his family out the back door and into his waiting limousine. Chase held Laura's elbow, allowing Rafe, Cam and his father to shield Tyler from anyone who might be watching. With the revelations about Brent's parentage, Laura had exhibited remarkable restraint. She hadn't said much during the meeting with Bradley, keeping her thoughts about the Senator and Chase to herself.

The Senator wearily leaned back into the plush leather seat and directed his comment to Chase. "I've done as you asked."

"Done what?" Cam asked, ducking his head as he took a seat across from Laura, Chase and the Senator.

"Baited the trap," Chase explained. "I've asked Dad to casually mention to the sheriff, Lance, Judge Stewart and now Bradley that Tyler, Laura and I will be up in the high pasture late tomorrow afternoon."

Chase hoped the killer wouldn't be able to resist attacking them in the isolated area. And if the killer showed, his prepared family could uncover the murderer's identity, capture him and bring him to justice. Nothing less would bring closure.

Laura chewed her bottom lip. "We won't be there looking for missing cows?"

Chase willed her to look into his eyes and see how much he cared about her. "I want the killer to come after me. You and Tyler won't be there at all."

"I'm not letting you go alone," Tyler growled.

"Neither am I." Laura refused to meet his gaze, looking at a spot over his left shoulder. She held up her hand, signaling she wasn't done speaking. "If the killer doesn't find all of us, he may not attack and the plan won't work. So we'll all go. And the Senator and the sheriff, Cam, Rafe and my dad will watch our backs."

Chase refused to let her risk her life. "You aren't going. I won't risk you getting hurt."

"It's a little late for that."

He winced at the pain in her tone and from the determined look in her eyes, he knew he'd alienate her further if he insisted she stay behind. So Chase didn't argue. He'd just make sure his family was ready to move out before Laura arrived.

She gave him a curious look when he didn't argue further, as if she knew he'd given in too easily.

He heaved a sigh of relief when she turned to the Senator. "Chase and I were at the courthouse earlier and found ten acres of Sutton land that Bradley donated to the county as a park over twenty years ago."

"And...?" The Senator looked calm, but Chase had felt him tense beside him.

"Come on, Dad. You've repeatedly told us that Suttons don't sell the land. Ever."

"He didn't sell it," Laura said softly. "The documentary stamps on the deed show the property was a gift.''

''Bradley did you a favor?'' Rafe asked.

''Wasn't Bradley's family killed about twenty years ago?'' Cam's tone was mild but it whipped through the car, flaying their nerves raw. His instinct for putting pieces of information together was a gift that would have been the envy of any homicide detective.

The Senator closed his eyes and then opened them. ''I guess today is the day for old secrets. Twenty years ago, I'd just decided to throw my hat into the ring for the Senate race. I was out late with Stewart, Perkins and Noel, playing poker, drinking and planning my campaign.''

''You were drinking?'' Rafe asked.

The Senator shuddered. ''I haven't touched a drop since that night. We broke up the game early on account of the rain and I drove home alone. It was raining so hard, the drops spattered the windshield. sideways. Thunder rattled the floorboards of the car and lightning lit the skies like the fires of hell. No one should have been out driving. And Mark Bradley's wife was speeding. She ran through a traffic light that was out from the storm, plowed into my car. She and the children died instantly.''

Chase knew there was more to the horrible tragedy. The Senator's name had never been publicly connected to the accident.

''I called Noel, who I'd just helped get elected sheriff. We both knew my political career would be over before it started if news of the accident and my drinking leaked. He convinced me to keep silent. Noel wrote up the report as a one-car accident and

I went home. But Bradley was suspicious. He snooped around and matched paint chips from the fender of his wife's car to the dent in mine and went to Noel with his suspicions. Noel called me and I got rid of the car. Bradley had no proof.''

"And you gave Bradley the land to keep quiet?" Laura asked.

"It was understood between us but never spoken."

"I don't understand why ten acres of land would keep Bradley quiet," Chase said. "Especially since he didn't even keep the bribe but donated the land to a park."

"He never had the proof to make his accusations stand, so it wasn't really a bribe," the Senator tried to explain. "I have no idea why he donated the land. Maybe he felt as if he'd accepted blood money and wanted to do something good in his children's names."

The Senator frowned, the sadness, regret and pain in his eyes evident. "You have to understand, even though Bradley's wife hit my car, I was at fault because I'd been drinking. If the news had gone public, the press would have smeared my name. I'm not proud of what I did, but at the time I thought I was protecting my future. Our family's future."

Chase glanced from one brother's face to another, seeing understanding and sorrow and pain. He wondered if his own expression looked as bleak as theirs. Surprisingly it was Laura who found the words to comfort his father.

She leaned over and patted the Senator's hand. "You shouldn't feel guilty. It wasn't your fault that the power was out or that she was driving too fast."

"I never saw her car until she broadsided me."

"Nothing you could have done would have saved them," Laura insisted.

"That's what Bradley said when I told him what really happened that night."

Rafe whistled. "You told him?"

"I had nothing to lose after my car was destroyed. And…I wanted to ease my conscience—if I could."

"Did he believe you?" Cam asked.

"I don't know. He seemed preoccupied with the reason why his wife was out late that night."

"But if he thinks you destroyed his family, then no doubt he'd have more than enough reason to destroy yours," Laura said.

"His wife was leaving him," the Senator told them. "She was having an affair with Stewart who was his law partner back then."

"Did Bradley know?" Laura asked.

The Senator shrugged. "What you may also not realize is that Bradley's wife was Lance's sister. So if the killer is after my family because of the car accident—"

Laura's eyes darkened to a Caribbean blue. "The killer could be Bradley, my attorney and her husband—"

"Or Lance, her brother," added Tyler.

"Or Judge Stewart, her lover?" said Rafe.

Laura frowned. "You think our killer waited twenty years for revenge, trying to blame Tyler's attempted murder on me because I was already a suspect in Brent's murder?"

The Senator nodded. "It's possible that was the opportunity he was waiting for."

Hearing the tangled web of connections, Chase

realized that he wished he and Laura could start clean. He didn't want any more lies between them. He didn't want to place her in danger by taking her onto that mountain tomorrow—yet he sensed if he left her behind, he'd lose her forever because she'd never forgive him another deception.

And he decided lying to her about what time they'd leave tomorrow was wrong. He wouldn't countenance more deception and lies—not even to protect her. Laura was a fine, strong woman—the best—and she deserved his honesty. Always.

He'd just have to make sure she was well protected.

"I DON'T KNOW how you talked me into riding up here alone with you." Laura glanced over at Chase, who sat tall and straight in the saddle. He was so in tune with his mount, he guided the horse with his knees and barely used the reins at all. Despite his alertness, eyes scanning the horizon and missing little, he had an ease about him that could only be acquired after spending a lifetime on horseback.

Chase belonged out here among the vast mountains and verdant pastures the same way birds belonged in the sky and trout belonged in mountain lakes. This land was his heritage, the future he wanted to share with his son. And she couldn't think of a better way for Keith to grow up.

Although Chase planned to check out the pastureland where they would set the trap, Laura had no idea if their plan would work. Would the killer come after them? And would it be Lance? Bradley or Judge Stewart? She had no idea. She only hoped it would be over soon.

Chase had convinced her that they needed time alone and they'd left at dawn, hours before the rest of his family. Chase wanted to check out the land and look for good places for his family to hide while they protected their backs. But they had several hours before they'd reach the high pasture. In the meantime, she took pleasure that he'd invited her to join him and had agreed to accompany him without hesitation.

His tone teased, telling her he'd like to do so much more than caress her with words. "You came with me because I'm irresistible."

"And modest, too." He *was* irresistible but she didn't want to admit it to him, maybe not even to herself. Ever since Laura had seen Tyler walk into Bradley's office, she'd been trying to move past her anger and feelings of betrayal, sorting through her confusion, deciding what she really wanted. And needed.

She didn't want to be one of those women who blindly followed a man no matter how he trampled her feelings. Yet she refused to be so rigid and un-forgiving that she lost the only man she'd ever loved. Chase wasn't perfect. He was living, breathing flesh and blood with a heart as big as this valley. He wasn't secretive by nature and it must have been difficult for him to follow his father's wishes and lie to her. He'd apologized. What more did she want?

Hell! She wasn't perfect, either. Chase had stood by her even when they'd both thought she'd killed his brother. Her parents already treated Chase like a son. Keith adored him. She had no idea why she couldn't pull down the mountain that had seemed to emerge between them.

Could it be that she needed the Suttons to fully accept her? She had to face that that might never happen. That they had all lied to her about Tyler's faked death still hurt her deeply. They'd treated her like an outsider, and yet they'd been mighty nice to her when she was the sole suspect in both Brent's murder and Tyler's suspected murder. She and Chase were adult enough to build their own lives without his family's approval. Yet as close as the Suttons were to one another, she didn't want to force Chase to choose between his family and her.

After two hours of riding toward the high pastures with no signs of the missing cattle, Chase drew his mount to a halt alongside a tumbling mountain stream beside a huge outcrop of rock. The sun-filled sky of morning had become overcast, with the storm clouds that hovered over the mountains closing in on them, leaving them in a cocoon of intimacy as if they were the only people on the planet. Chase removed his bedroll from behind the cantle, spread it on the creek's bank while Laura removed their lunch from her backpack.

Chase leaned over her and helped himself to a fried chicken drumstick. "You've been quiet. What are you thinking?"

"About us."

She loved watching his white teeth tear great big bites out of the chicken, then neatly chew and swallow the prize. She liked that he didn't press her to speak before she knew her own mind. But most of all she enjoyed the freedom she felt when he was with her. He treated her as an equal, even if he had to suppress his over protective tendencies.

She sipped water out of a plastic bottle, letting the cool liquid trickle down her parched throat. "I thought you were going to try to sneak up here without me."

"The thought occurred to me," he admitted, surprising her with his candor, eyes darkening as he focused on her.

She picked up a deviled egg and offered it to him. "What made you decide to bring me along?"

"I said I would." He paused, bit and swallowed the egg, smacking his lips in quiet appreciation. "And I won't lie to you again."

"Even to protect your family?"

"You and Keith are my family."

She could feel the intensity beaming off him like stray sunbeams breaking through a foggy mist and shooting heat straight to her core. She had to hold herself back from throwing herself into his arms. But words needed to be said and once she touched him, she wouldn't be able to think.

She had to ask the question while she could still remember her doubts, before his sensuality overwhelmed her. "And what will the rest of the Suttons think about us?"

"It doesn't matter."

Not the answer she'd expected. Her heart sped at the thought he would follow his own feelings, going against the family he loved. But she didn't want him to have to choose between the Suttons and her and his son. "Of course, it matters. Out here neighbors and friends are important, often the difference between extinction and survival. Family is most important of all.''

Chase's brow wrinkled in puzzlement even as he reached for her hand. ''I thought you liked my brothers?''

''I do. I think your brothers are wonderful.''

''So it's the Senator you don't like?''

''You've got it backward. He doesn't like me.''

''Huh?'' Chase's frown deepened and he leaned forward as if he couldn't figure out where she was coming from. ''Even when my father thought you'd murdered Brent, the Senator's gone out of his way to remain fair. He never objected when you made bail. He also requested that the sheriff delay your arrest after Tyler's accident. And I've never heard him say a harsh word against you.''

Laura heard the honesty in Chase's words and wondered if her own doubts had clouded her thinking. Living next to the Suttons could give anyone an inferiority complex. And she wondered if she'd read disapproval from the Senator when none was intended because she'd felt guilty. But she had no reason to feel guilt anymore.

At the realization that the only thing stopping her from going to Chase and accepting him with her whole soul was her own self-doubt, her heart lifted and she scooted closer to him. He made room beside him, turned onto his back on the bedroll, his hands clasped behind his head to watch the puffy gray storm clouds with charcoal underbellies hurl long shadows across the overcast sky.

The imminent summer storm didn't worry her. They'd both brought slickers and she turned her attention from the sky back to Chase. Gently, she placed her palm against his jaw until his eyes met hers. "I love you."

"I know." His mouth twisted into a satisfied line of masculine triumph. "I've been waiting for you to figure it out."

She punched his shoulder lightly. "What do you mean, you know?"

"Cam told me." It was her turn to be confused. "He said you wouldn't have been so angry with me unless you cared."

"Your brother is a very wise man." She snuggled closer, letting her fingers trail down his neck into the open V of his shirt. "Maybe Cam should have told you that when a woman declares her love, she'd like the man to tell her he loves her back."

"Cam didn't mention that—" Chase's eyes glinted with mischief "—but Rafe suggested I kiss you until you changed your mind."

She leaned over him until their lips were a mere centimeter apart. "So what are you waiting for?"

"I'm trying to decide."

"Decide what?"

"What to do first. Should I kiss you or tell you I love you?"

He kissed her nose as the first raindrops spattered beside them and plopped into the babbling creek. "Decisions." He kissed her cheek. "Decisions." He kissed her chin. "Delicious." He brushed his lips against hers. "I love you, Laura. I always have and I always will."

"How touching." A cold metal rod prodded Laura in the back. Beneath her, Chase's body went rigid and his eyes turned stormy as he stared over her shoulder.

Laura looked up to see two men she didn't recognize holding guns pointed at her and Chase. The men's faces were weather-beaten and lined, their fingers callused and she suspected they'd just found their cattle rustlers. The creek's soft gurgle had muffled their footsteps while the rock outcropping had allowed the men to sneak up on them unseen.

"Tie them up. Did you think I wouldn't have you watched? Wouldn't know that you came up here early?" Heart thudding at the familiar voice tinged with anger and victory, she looked at the third man as he strode around the rocky outcrop. Mark Bradley!

The man she'd been confiding to, who knew every major and minor point of her case had set her up. And she already knew why. Through all these years, Bradley had blamed the Senator for his family's death and Laura's misfortune had given him the opportunity for revenge.

Bradley had had twenty years for his bitterness to brew inside him and she doubted they could make him see reason now. She'd recalled the glint in his eyes when he'd dug up dirt on the Senator, his triumphant tone as he threw the newspaper headlines down, revealing the Senator's secrets. He'd gone too far for mere words to stop him from taking his revenge. A sickening chill shivered down her spine as one of the men tied her wrists together behind her back while the other man tied Chase who had the sense not to struggle with Bradley's gun pointed at them.

Chase's plan to draw out the enemy had worked out all too well. Her attorney had taken the bait. Only he'd shown up before they could set the trap.

Chapter Thirteen

One look at the merciless glint in Bradley's eyes and Chase realized that crossing the killer was about as dangerous as walking in quicksand. And he damned himself for failing to remain alert, putting Laura in danger. He should have anticipated the killer might have had them watched.

Just as Bradley's man tied his wrists, the skies above opened. Hands tied behind his back, outnumbered, with no chance of regaining the rifle in his saddle, Chase knew their odds of survival weren't any good.

Laura's wide eyes and pale face showed she fully understood their dire predicament. Now that Bradley had revealed his identity, he'd never voluntarily release them.

The sky darkened to black, the mountains above them and the valley below disappearing in thick storm clouds. Lightning crackled overhead and thunder boomed, sending the horses into a wild stampede down the mountain.

Bradley cursed at his men. "Don't let the horses get away!"

But it was too late. Hopefully the Senator and his

brothers would intercept the horses on the way up, realize there had been trouble and approach with caution. While Chase worried over his father and brothers, he suspected that the horses leaving them on foot had been a stroke of luck. It limited Bradley's options.

"Let's go." One of the men prodded Laura with his rifle.

She tossed her dripping hair from her eyes. "Where are you taking us?"

Without answering, the man shoved her forward and Chase's anger surged at her rough treatment. If only his hands were free. If only he and Laura hadn't stopped in the lee of those huge rocks. If only he'd kept his mind on business. If only—

A rifle barrel slammed into his shoulder and almost knocked him off his feet. "Move."

Ignoring the pain, Chase staggered, caught the cowboy's eye. "Bradley intends to kill us."

Bradley shoved the man aside and backhanded Chase across the face. "Shut up!"

What Bradley lacked in muscles, he made up for in weight. The man might spend his days in court but he hefted power in his punch. A cut opened on Chase's cheek and bled onto his shirt. Pain only fueled his determination. Clearly Bradley hadn't shared his intentions with his hired hands. If Chase could cause dissent in the ranks, any blows he took could be worth the pain he'd suffer.

Chase spoke loudly to be heard above the storm. "Bradley's already wanted for attempted murder. He's going away to jail for a long—"

Bradley's fist slammed into Chase's chest, knocking the wind out of him. His lungs strained for air but he couldn't inhale.

Beside him Laura picked up on his plan and made it hers, shouting at their captors through pelting rain. "Bradley may kill us but he won't get away with our murders. He's going to be caught and you'll go—"

The two hands might have been reluctant to strike a woman but Bradley had no such compunctions. His meaty hand slapped Laura across the face, sending her falling to her knees.

"Leave her alone," Chase growled as he fought for breath, refusing to let Bradley see the shudder of horror that gripped him. He vowed to get even, at the same time wishing she wouldn't draw attention to herself.

But she kept shouting, "You'll spend the rest of your lives in jail. Chase's father is a powerful senator. He'll hunt you down. Make you pay. Cage you like animals. And you know what they do to men in jail, don't you?"

Chase signaled her to be silent and when she ignored him, he finally managed an earsplitting shout. "Laura!"

"I said shut up!" Bradley let out a piercing curse, drew back his booted foot to kick her. Chase launched himself, throwing his body between them and taking the blow on his hip with a grunt.

The ranch hand looked from Laura and Chase on the muddy ground to Bradley. "I didn't sign on for no murder."

"You didn't say his daddy was a senator," protested the second hand. "You said we'd only tie them up until we rustled the cattle."

"It makes no difference." Bradley's voice was frighteningly calm. "The Senator and his sons will ride up the mountain to find them and we'll kill the whole cursed family. We won't leave witnesses. We won't leave even one Sutton to come after us. When we're through here, we'll kill the baby, too. Don't want him growing up to ruin my old age."

"Mister, I've a sudden hankering to sniff Gulf breezes and roll my tail south. I signed on as a handyman with a runnin' iron. I didn't mind muddying up a few tracks or cutting fences to help you out or spying on the family doings, but murder makes me nervous. I don't kill men, women or babies." In disgust, the man turned his gun on Bradley. "We'll settle for the cattle we already rustled and show you our boot heels now."

Laura rolled to her side, bent her legs beneath her and rose to her feet, her face pleading for the men to take them, too. "Please—"

Chase shook his head, stopping her plea. Bradley's round face reddened in sizzling anger and Chase didn't want the man to erupt in violence. Not while he had a gun in his hand.

Escape on their minds, the attorney's hired hands backed away and around the rock. Chase thought he heard the sounds of galloping hoofbeats but couldn't be sure. While the men hadn't stayed to carry out Bradley's orders, Chase knew they wouldn't be calling in the law, either. When men like that hit the breeze for a healthier climate they didn't stop to chat with the sheriff.

The storm had whipped itself into a fury of hissing rain and spitting wind, transforming the pastoral mountainside into a bleak landscape of violence. For a moment, while Bradley was distracted by the weather, Chase considered kicking the gun from Bradley's hand but his position was poor and gave him little leverage.

Besides, the wily attorney moved away, using Laura as a shield and holding the gun to her neck but his orders were directed at Chase. "Get moving and if you turn around to even look at us, she's dead."

Chase didn't doubt the attorney's capacity for evil and his heart constricted in fear for Laura. Bradley was keeping them alive for only one reason. He wanted to kill the rest of the Suttons as they attempted to rescue Laura and Chase. Chase wouldn't let that happen. Obviously the man blamed the Senator for the loss of his family in the car accident. And now he intended to get even by killing off the Senator's family. Chase had to find a way to stop him. He deliberately left a trail for anyone who might be looking to follow, marking soft spots in the mud and breaking branches as he passed by.

Chase had no choice but to obey Bradley's command to keep going. Slowly, he pushed to his feet, knowing that Bradley would only keep them alive until he had no further need for them. And if his ultimate goal was to kill the Senator's family, using Chase to lure the Suttons into gun range, then Bradley had no real reason to keep Laura alive at all.

Chase needed the man off balance. Despite Bradley's proficiency with a gun, the man worked in an office. No doubt the stormy weather was bothering him much more than he'd admit and Chase sought to use the elements to his advantage.

"There's a cabin about another two miles up the mountain. Is that where we're headed?"

"We'll wait for your family there," Bradley agreed to his suggestion without suspicion.

Walking with his hands tied behind his back, up a steep slope, in the slippery mud, wasn't easy. Chase's cheek stung, his shoulder ached and his hip burned like fire, but he ignored the pain, instead focusing on marking the trail while he reviewed his options. The attorney was already furious and on edge. He couldn't afford to stoke Bradley's anger.

Think.

Chase knew this mountain, but with the rain sluicing down he was wishing he'd grown fins instead of feet. Although they'd come up here early to assess line-of-sight hiding spots to ambush a villain, he'd played all over the acreage as a child, explored as a teenager, herded cattle up in the spring and down in the fall. He knew every nook and cranny, every precipice, but how could he use the knowledge to his advantage without agitating Bradley's suspicions?

Behind him, Chase heard Laura tumble and winced as she grunted with pain. Frustrated, he didn't dare look back, didn't dare to turn and offer encouragement. All he could do was slow his footsteps and pray Bradley didn't notice.

"Get up or I'll leave you here."

At the threat to Laura, Chase tensed, ready to throw himself at Bradley and his gun, but the action proved unnecessary. From the corner of his eyes, he saw Laura struggle from her stomach to her knees to her feet. Somehow Laura had found the strength to go on.

Rage at their vulnerability heated his temper, but Laura's teeth chattering behind him reminded him to stay in control. Instead of recalling how easily he could warm her, instead of aching to take her into his arms and whisper words of encouragement in her ear, he had to figure a way to save them. She'd coolly kept her mouth shut as if sensing Chase had a plan. He had every confidence Laura would pick up on his signal.

In the desperate reaches of his mind, Chase had come up with an idea, but knowing Laura would understand and counting on her chilled leg muscles to have the strength required were two different skills. Could she make her cold, bruised and aching legs run a hundred-yard dash?

His best scheme, if it worked, would only weaken Bradley, wear him down and make him uncomfortable. Hopefully Bradley would suffer enough so that when Chase made a final stand, the man would be slow to react to danger.

Chase stopped in the shelter of a boulder to give Laura a chance to rest and spoke without looking back. "How you holding up back there?"

"I didn't call for a halt," Bradley sneered.

"We have to talk."

"Keep moving."

Chase held perfectly still. "Either we climb to high ground or we risk drowning in a flash flood."

Bradley's voice whined with his temper. "So take the high ground."

Chase tilted his chin, gesturing toward the rocks above. "We can't climb with our hands tied."

"Then we'll risk drowning because I'm not untying you, Sutton."

Chase had suspected as much. Time to put plan B in motion and pray.

Without another word of protest, Chase picked his path carefully, knowing a few feet could make the difference between success and failure. If he altered his direction at the last minute, Bradley might be suspicious.

As they cleared a hummock, Chase took stock in their direction and made a minor adjustment in their heading. Peering through the rain, he spied the tree he'd been searching for and used it as a beacon. Bradley was panting and Chase was counting on the fact that the heavyset Bradley couldn't run uphill as quickly as Laura.

The conical beehive hung from the branch just where Chase remembered, low enough for boys to smoke up the hive and steal honey but high enough to catch a tall man in the face if he wasn't wise enough to duck. Chase suspected Bradley was watching Chase and Laura and maybe looking at where he planted his feet in the slick grass and mud. The man had no reason to raise his face to the heavens. That would cost him.

As Chase walked under the hive, he knocked it with a blow from his head, disturbing the bees. He tried to make his voice sound surprised and alarmed. "Damn, we've run into a beehive! Laura, run."

Several bees stung Chase and he knew several more would sting Laura. Gamely running as best she could with her hands tied behind her back, she kept up the pace, slipping and sliding but running forward in jerky strides.

It took Bradley a moment to comprehend what had happened. His instinct to pursue his captives left him flailing and puffing behind. Chase and Laura couldn't outrace Bradley's gun, but with any luck the bees would attack in force, stinging the attorney who was closest to the hive.

Bradley bellowed like a fresh cut bull. Chase hoped the man suffered enough beestings to render him unconscious. However Bradley had the devil's luck, cursing and swatting but he never let go of his gun, managing to remain upright.

Moments later, Bradley's gunshot blast had Chase rooting his feet in the ground, yet not quite daring to turn around. Oh, God! Had Bradley shot Laura? Had he pushed the man too far? Or did he suspect Chase had deliberately led him into the hive?

Fear that Laura was injured or worse tightened Chase's throat until he could barely speak. "Laura?"

"Still here," she panted.

Relief washed over him in waves, leaving him weak and yet hopeful. They were still alive and Bradley had to be hurting.

"Hold up, right now or I'll plug you both," Bradley ordered between ragged gulps of air.

Lightning flashed and Chase glimpsed Bradley's bee-stung face. Jowls already swelling, one eye almost closed, Bradley looked limp as a worn-out fiddle string. Unfortunately, he still had a gun. And while he might move slower than a snail on crutches, he was weasel smart.

Chase didn't move a muscle. He kept his head bowed, unwilling to risk letting Bradley look into his eyes for fear he'd see a glint of triumph.

Bradley spoke through swollen lips. "How much farther to the cabin?"

"It's right up ahead." Chase wondered if he dared bypass the shelter and keep Bradley walking in circles until he tired out the attorney. If Chase intended to disarm the man, it would be better to have a clear sight of his target.

He led them to the crude cabin the ranch hands used when needed. It was dark enough inside to slow down a bat. But the Suttons kept the place stocked with basic provisions and emergency supplies, and the solid roof and walls would protect them from the elements.

Inside, Chase waited for Laura and Bradley to follow. "There's a lantern and matches by the woodstove."

He'd hoped Bradley would put down the gun to light the stove but he took out a penlight, flicked it on and motioned Chase to the floor by the far wall. Then he untied Laura. "Light the lantern and remember I'm keeping the gun on Sutton."

Laura rubbed her hands. "My fingers are numb."

Bradley raised the gun. "Do it."

Laura fumbled with the matches for what seemed a long time. Finally she lit the lantern and the welcome glow banished the darkness to the cabin's corners. Before Bradley could retie Laura's hands, she hurried to Chase and flung her arms around his chest. Dripping wet and icy cold, she curled in his heat like a cat in the sun.

He leaned forward and whispered in her ear. "Be ready."

Mouth dropping, Bradley sagged against the cabin's far wall, seemingly oblivious to them, looking pretty bad. Chase counted at least ten stings on the man's face alone. The bees had weakened him and Chase could see he was fighting to remain alert.

Bradley still kept a firm grip on the gun, however, pointing the weapon at Laura. "Fix me something hot to drink."

Laura looked at Chase for instructions. "There's a wood-burning stove by the sink. Hopefully it's already filled with dry wood. Supplies are in the cupboard over there." He gestured with his chin.

Laura stood, clearly reluctant to leave him. But she had a determined glint in her eyes that had Chase alarmed. He didn't want her trying any heroics. She might have the heart of a lioness, but she was no match for Bradley and his gun.

When Laura yanked open a drawer so hard that the contents clanged to the floor, Bradley moved nimbly. At the sight of several knives, he lunged to his feet and waved the gun wildly, looking mad enough to eat the devil with his horns on. "Get back."

Chase didn't like the feral glint in Bradley's eyes, almost as if he realized he couldn't fight the bee-stings much longer. As Bradley kicked the knives to the far side of the cabin, Chase eased his way to his feet.

But Bradley must have caught a hint of motion. He spun around, his face meaner than a boar as he pointed the gun at Laura. Thighs bursting with effort, Chase darted across the cabin, focusing his eyes on the gun. With instinctive timing, Chase kicked the man's wrist, sending the gun flying across the room. "Run, Laura."

As the two men collided, flesh pounded flesh and Chase hoped Laura had fled, hoped she could find her way down the mountain, hoped she could warn his family about Bradley. She had to get away.

With his hands tied behind him, Chase tackled Bradley low and hard and the two men fell, Chase landing on top. Using the weapons he had, Chase pounded his knees into the other man's side, butted his forehead into the man's swollen nose.

With a roar, Bradley rolled away, scraping along the floor, his hands flailing for the gun. Chase tried to kick him in the temple. Missed and struck a shoulder instead.

Laura needed time to escape and bring back help. Chase had to slow him down.

With hands free to help him rise, Bradley scampered to his knees before Chase did. Catching Chase off balance, he shoved Chase's shoulder hard, spinning him. And then Bradley's big hands closed around Chase's throat, cutting off his air.

Dazed from lack of air, he held on to one thought. He couldn't pass out. Laura needed him. Chase bucked, twisted, contorted beneath the deadly pressure of Bradley's fingers around his throat, trying to free himself from the killer. But he failed. His ears roared and blackness closed in.

"Let him go!"

Chase heard Laura's scream through a dark tunnel of waning consciousness. Suddenly his throat was free. He sucked huge gulps of air into his oxygen-starved body and slowly, his vision returned.

Laura hadn't left to go for help. Somehow, she'd scooped up Bradley's gun.

In the next instant, the door slammed open and the Senator, the sheriff and his brothers burst in. Distracted by the interruption, Laura glanced away from Bradley. And he took advantage. Bradley lunged at her and the gun she held. For the space of a heartbeat, man and woman struggled over the weapon. A shot fired. Laura screamed and fell.

Barely conscious, instinct forced Chase to rise, scramble across the room and cover her with his body. If Bradley got off another shot, he'd have to go through Chase.

Sick that she'd stayed to help him, furious that she'd been hurt and might be bleeding to death beneath him, Chase waited for his family to subdue Bradley, determined that no one would get another shot at her. Lack of oxygen had made the world go fuzzy, but he had to keep his Laura safe.

A fist pounded Chase's shoulder. "Let me up."

Powerful hands pulled Chase to his feet. While Rafe untied him, Chase frowned at Laura. She was pale, drenched and lying unmoving on the floor, just staring at him with tears running down her cheeks. "I didn't know what to do but I couldn't leave you alone. I was so scared he'd shoot you."

As soon as Chase's hands were free, he knelt and gently pulled her into his arms. "Laura?"

"I'm okay," she told him through her tears.

"But—" Chase didn't want to take his gaze off her. He could barely believe she was alive, not hurt. But finally he turned his head and saw Bradley's body.

Cam squatted by the attorney, checking for a pulse. "You shot him in the heart, Sheriff."

The shot he'd heard had been the sheriff shooting Bradley. The gun Laura had been struggling to keep hadn't fired and Chase turned back to Laura, relieved that she wouldn't have to live with the death of a man on her conscience. "You saved my life."

"I didn't know what to do but I couldn't leave you alone. I couldn't go for help and leave you tied up with that monster."

"Shh. You did great."

The sheriff walked over to Chase. "My deputies rounded up two shady-looking characters on the way down the mountain. Before this is over, we may even find the missing cattle."

Chase didn't care about the cattle. All he wanted was to hold Laura close.

Her voice trembled. "Bradley was going to kill us. All of us. Even Keith."

Chase smoothed back her hair and gathered her into his lap. "He'll never hurt anyone again."

The Suttons and Laura rode back down the mountain through the storm. With lightning and thunder dogging their footsteps, all conversation was saved until they reached the Sutton stable where Laura's parents were waiting with Keith.

Chase helped Laura dismount.

Chase's brothers and father and her parents and Keith crowded around them. The Senator took her hand and Chase swallowed hard at the look of pride on his father's face. The Senator couldn't have been more proud of Laura if she'd been his daughter. "I want to thank you for all you have done for our family. And I want to apologize for Brent's—"

Laura held tight to the Senator's hand. "I'm sorry I left Brent lying on the barn floor. Maybe if I'd run for help, he might still be—"

The Senator shook his head. "We all make mistakes. And I've made plenty. But there's one I can rectify. Chase tried to tell me but I wouldn't listen. The ranch is too big, too much trouble for one man alone to run. I want my children to have time to devote to their families as well as to their work. The future is with my grandchildren and I want them all to live out here. Or visit often. So I'm dividing the acreage among you four boys to pass on to your own children.''

''I think it would make a fine wedding present,'' Cam said, smiling at Chase and Laura.

Rafe let out a whistle. ''He's getting married?''

''I haven't asked her yet,'' Chase murmured, cuddling Laura against his chest.

''I recommend you do so before I become a grandfather again.'' The Senator smiled, taking any sting from his words.

''I second that,'' said Laura's father.

Tyler tried to frown but his mouth twisted in amusement. ''Chase, so help me if you don't propose right now, I'll snatch her out of your arms and marry her myself.''

''What's po-pose?'' Keith asked.

Anna cuddled her grandson. ''It means marriage, sweetie-pie.''

Rafe slapped Chase on the shoulder. ''Hey, you're almost on your knees. Ask her.''

Chase swallowed back a chuckle as heat rose to Laura's cheeks. ''So we're all in agreement?''

At the nods and shouts of encouragement, Chase smoothed Laura's hair off her face, enjoying the feel of her arms wrapped around his neck so tight he knew she never wanted to let go. ''Give me some room, guys. You're crowding my style.''

''What style?'' Rafe muttered.

"Maybe she'll agree to take him off our hands if we leave them alone," Cam suggested.

"I want to stay," Keith piped in.

Clearly no one was going anywhere in this rain. Chase had imagined proposing to her in some fancy restaurant with flowers and a ring, not in the stable. Especially not surrounded by family. The setting couldn't have been more unromantic, but Laura didn't seem to mind. And he didn't have to think twice.

"Marry me, sweetheart?"

Her eyes brimmed with love. "Yes!"

"Imagine that, she loves him." Rafe snorted.

Laura's mother's eyes shined with tears as she shared a look of love with her husband over Keith's head.

Tyler shook his head and spoke to Laura. "Women have strange tastes. Are you sure you wouldn't prefer—"

Cam elbowed Tyler, effectively silencing him, then rocked back on his heels and folded his arms across his chest. He smiled down at Laura and Chase with satisfaction.

"Laura, welcome to the family." The Senator clapped Chase on the back. "Hurry up and kiss her, son. I only have one request."

Laura's gaze went from Chase to his father. "What's that, Senator?"

"This time I'd like a granddaughter."

Chase eagerly kissed Laura again. "Yes, sir. One baby girl, coming right up."

Epilogue

Damn the Sutton luck! As one file after another fed the flames, years of planning the Suttons' downfall went up in smoke. In the burning files, research carefully garnered revealed family skeletons, family secrets that should have set brother against brother and father against sons.

But Bradley had failed. Tyler had survived. And the Sutton family had grown by one. No matter. There were other ways to bring down the family. Secrets to be used against them. All in their proper time.

Together the Suttons appeared strong. But one by one they would suffer and die, their dreams turning to ashes. The father, his sons, their wives and their spawn—all would pay. The high and mighty would not only fall, they would suffer before their ultimate defeat.

But who would be next? One file opened and the hand holding it paused above the flames. Seeds planted long ago could be coaxed to bear fruit. Divide the family and conquer it. Was it possible? Yes.

On the vast Sutton estate the family was well-protected. Almost out of reach. But one brother had made his way alone in the world. Dr. Cameron Sutton had married into money. But money wouldn't save him. He lived back east, separate from his brothers, away from his family roots. And that would be his undoing....

We hope you enjoyed
CRADLE WILL ROCK,
book one of Susan Kearney's
new Harlequin Intrigue series,
THE SUTTON BABIES.
Please look for book two,
LITTLE BOYS BLUE (HI #590, 11/00)
next month.

For a sneak preview of
LITTLE BOYS BLUE,
turn the page....

Chapter One

"Don't be silly, Alexa," her cousin Sandra Sutton lectured. "You can watch the twins for the five minutes it'll take me to fetch us hot dogs and coffee."

Seeking to halt a rising sense of unease, Alexa Whitfield risked insulting her cousin by attempting to refuse. "I don't—"

"Know anything about babies," Sandra finished her sentence for her, an indication of how many times Alexa had used that particular excuse to avoid holding and feeding Flynn and Jason over the past few days of her visit.

Determined not to show her trepidation, Alexa neatly folded the *Boston News* and set the paper beside her on the park bench with a forced smile. "*I'll* get coffee."

"For Pete's sake. The twins are sleeping." Sandra stood, handed her the diaper bag filled with baby paraphernalia, beating Alexa to a clean getaway. Sandra's fashionable heels clicked along the pavement, but after a few steps she turned back with a smile of encouragement. "You'll never learn to enjoy kids if you aren't willing to try."

"By the time you get back, I'll be an expert."
Despite her inner turmoil, Alexa made her voice
lighthearted.

"Just don't drop them," Sandra instructed as she
fluffed her auburn hair with her hand.

"As if I didn't know that," Alexa grumbled.

Alexa Whitfield could determine a genuine
Picasso from a fake at twenty paces, but if Flynn or
Jason so much as burped, she wouldn't know what
to do. Not that she didn't think the twins were ador-
able. She did. Not that she didn't want to scoop them
up and bury her nose in their baby-soft skin. She'd
love to.

However fate had decreed that Alexa could never
be a mommy. Some women couldn't stay on a diet,
others didn't have the discipline to exercise regularly, some suffered from insomnia. Alexa couldn't
bear children but didn't dwell on her inability. Not
when life had so much else to offer.

Sandra had the love of her adoring husband, Dr.
Cameron Sutton and the twins; Alexa had a passion
for her work and a life most women would envy.
Purchasing museum quality art sent her to Rio during Carnivale, Paris in the spring and New York
City in the fall. She'd been invited to the White
House for dinner, attended parties in Milan, London
and Rome. European royalty often sought her ad-
vice.

Alexa stared at the twins asleep in their strollers
and wished she had her sketch pad. She'd love to
capture the babies' rounded cheeks, the dimples, the
black hair they'd inherited from their brilliant father
and the contrasting fair skin from their mother.
Leaning down, Alexa tucked in the blanket by

Flynn's feet, smoothed back Jason's hair, surprised by the satisfaction she'd received in the tiny gesture.

A shrill scream brought Alexa's head snapping up from the stroller.

Sandra!

Dear God, the scream had sounded like her cousin. As people ran down the path Sandra had taken, Alexa's fear shifted into high gear. Since the plane crash that had taken both sets of parents when they were toddlers, the cousins had been raised together by their wealthy grandparents and Alexa loved Sandra like a sister.

Don't panic. Sandra would come walking around the bend any minute, juggling hot dogs and coffee, tossing her auburn hair back from her eyes, ready to tell Alexa about the excitement.

Two minutes later, a siren screamed and Flynn awakened—at least she thought it was Flynn. Alexa was still having trouble telling the boys apart. With wide, frightened eyes, he looked for his mother and when he couldn't find her, he started to cry until huge tears rolled down his face.

Awkwardly, but without hesitation, Alexa picked him up, but not before Jason awakened and also started to howl.

"Now what? I don't have four arms." At her words the babies' cries subsided and she returned Flynn to the stroller. If she hadn't been so worried over Sandra, she would have been pleased by how easily she'd comforted the boys.

"Where's your mother?" Alexa checked her watch and decided Sandra had been gone over ten minutes. Should she stay and wait? If Sandra returned to find Alexa and her babies gone would she worry?

Alexa decided to walk up the block to the corner hot dog stand and come straight back. Most likely she'd run into Sandra who had stopped to chat with an acquaintance.

Shoving the baby stroller into motion, she walked briskly down the sidewalk determined to give Sandra a piece of her mind for scaring her so. Palms sweaty, Alexa rounded the corner to see yellow police tape cordoning off a crime scene.

Heart pounding, fear hastening her footsteps, Alexa hurried until her pace almost reached a jog behind the baby stroller. Shoving her way through the crowd, she took one look at the victim's cap of auburn hair and Alexa's knees turned to jelly.

"Sandra!"

A cop noticed Alexa and jerked his thumb toward the pavement where her cousin was being loaded onto a stretcher. "You know this woman?"

"My cousin." Alexa swallowed hard at the huge amount of blood on the sidewalk.

"She was mugged with a baseball bat." The cop kindly took Alexa's arm. "They're sending her to Boston Memorial but..."

At the implication that Sandra might not survive long enough to reach the hospital, tears brimmed in Alexa's eyes. "Can I see her?"

A minute later Alexa was leaning over her cousin as the paramedics strapped in her cousin. "Sandra?"

At the sound of Alexa's voice, Sandra turned her head, her beautiful clear blue eyes clouded with pain. "Tell Cam I love him."

"You can tell him yourself. I'll call him and he'll be waiting at the hospital."

Sandra convulsed, her entire body shuddering, but she kept talking. "Promise me."

"Anything."

"My boys. Take care of them."

"You'll get better. *You'll* take care of them."

Sandra grabbed her hand with waning strength. "Don't let…the grandparents…raise them."

"Hang on, Sandra. Fight. You and Cameron will raise the boys."

"No boarding schools. No nannies."

"They have their mother," Alexa insisted.

Sandra grasped Alexa's hand, refusing to let the paramedics put her in the ambulance until she had an answer. "Promise me."

Tears clogged Alexa's throat. "I promise."

What can be stolen, forgotten, hidden, replaced, imitated—but never lost?

THE SECRET IS OUT!

HARLEQUIN®

I N T R I G U E®

presents

By day these agents are cowboys;
by night they are specialized
government operatives.
Men bound by love, loyalty and the law—
they've vowed to keep their missions
and identities confidential....

Harlequin Intrigue

Harlequin American Romance
(a special tie-in story)

HARLEQUIN®

Makes any time special ™